THE HOLY SPIRIT
IN THE LIFE OF
JESUS

Six Major Events
That Shaped His Life

Volume 1

Ken Stewart D.Min.

The Holy Spirit in the Life of Jesus

ISBN: 978-1-962102-58-2 (Paperback)
ISBN: 978-1-83663-350-1 (eBook)
Copyright © 2023 by Kennith E. Stewart, D.Min.

Unless otherwise noted, all Scriptures in this book are taken from the KING JAMES VERSION (KJV): KING JAMES VERSION, public domain.

Scripture quotations marked AMPC are taken from the Amplified® Bible, Copyright © 1954, 1958, 1962, 1964, 1965, 1987 by The Lockman Foundation. Used by permission.

Scripture quotations marked ERV are taken from the HOLY BIBLE: EASY-TO-READ VERSION © 2001 by World Bible Translation Center, Inc. and used by permission.

Scripture quotations marked ESV are taken from THE HOLY BIBLE, ENGLISH STANDARD VERSION® (ESV) Copyright© 2001 by Crossway, a publishing ministry of Good News Publishers. Used by permission.

Scripture quotations marked HCSB are taken from the HOLMAN CHRISTIAN STANDARD BIBLE (HCSB): copyright© 1999, 2000, 2002, 2003 by Holman Bible Publishers, Nashville, Tennessee. All rights reserved.

Scripture quotations marked ISV are taken from the Holy Bible: International Standard Version® Release 2.0. Copyright © 1996-2013 by the ISV Foundation. Used by permission of Davidson Press, LLC. ALL RIGHTS RESERVED INTERNATIONALLY.

Scripture quotations marked KJ21 are taken from The Holy Bible, 21st Century King James Version (KJ21®), Copyright © 1994, Deuel Enterprises, Inc., Gary, SD 57237, and used by permission.

Scripture quotations marked NCB taken from THE NEW CATHOLIC BIBLE. Copyright © 2019 Catholic Book Publishing Corp. Used by permission. All rights reserved.

Scripture quotations marked NIV are taken from THE HOLY BIBLE, NEW INTERNATIONAL VERSION ®. Copyright© 1973, 1978, 1984, 2011 by Biblica, Inc.™. Used by permission of Zondervan. All rights reserved worldwide.

Scripture quotations marked NKJV are taken from the NEW KING JAMES VERSION® (NKJV): Copyright© 1982 by Thomas Nelson, Inc. Used by permission. All rights reserved.

Scripture quotations marked NLT are taken from the Holy Bible, New Living Translation, copyright 1996, 2004. Used by permission of Tyndale House Publishers, Inc., Wheaton, Illinois 60189. All rights reserved.

Contents

Introduction

Did Jesus come to this planet fully prepared and equipped to do the job His Father had assigned Him to do? My guess is that many Christians would answer this question with a resounding yes. I believe they would be very wrong. Jesus needed to grow, learn and mature, both in natural things and in spiritual things. Now you know this book will be filled with things that are not typical. I will do my best to ensure it is solidly based on the Word of God.

I will give you some things to ponder. Jesus did things during the three years of His ministry that I have never done. These are things that I have never seen anyone else do. This very fact troubles me deeply. It is the reason I have written this book. If it has yet to dawn on you what I may be talking about, consider these statements by Jesus.

> *Believe me that I am in the Father, and the Father in me: or else believe me for the very works' sake. Verily, verily, I say unto you, He that believeth on me, the works that I do shall he do also; and greater works than these shall he do; because I go unto my Father. And whatsoever ye shall ask in my name, that will I do, that the Father may be glorified in the Son. (John 14:11-13 – KJV)*

There is not a shred of doubt in my mind and heart concerning who Jesus was and is. He is the Son of God. I believe in Him. I believe on Him, and any other way this can be said. It is the next part that troubles me. Not that Jesus said it, but why don't we see it happening repeatedly? Let's consider this in its obvious two parts.

Jesus said *the works that I do shall he do also*. The Greek translated **works** means an act, deed, or (a) thing done.[1] Well, there were a lot of things Jesus did. He opened blind eyes. He cleansed lepers. He raised the dead. As you recall, a man named Lazarus had been dead for four days and was buried. Jesus called his name, and Lazarus came back to life and came out of the tomb. How many times have you seen that done? For me, the answer is none! I have asked myself many times, why? I find it difficult to think of moving on to the next statement until I can come to grips with this one. We should all be doing what Jesus did.

It has been my privilege to see one lady who was born blind receive her sight. I have ministered to two different men who had been told they were blind in one eye and would never be able to see in that eye again. God healed them both, and their eye doctors confirmed it. The way I understand the statements Jesus made; these things should be happening all the time. There have been other remarkable documented healings and even miracles during my years of ministry.

I want to see thousands upon thousands of believers laying hands on people with every kind of sickness and see those sick people get well. Miracles should be everywhere. Great signs and wonders which have no logical explanation should be the rule of the day. This is the only way I can imagine the things Jesus said could be a reality. So, my quest is to discover why we have spent the past 2000 years coming up short.

For almost sixty years, I have been searching for answers. I have found the real root of the problem. It all goes back to our lack of understanding of this precious person we call Jesus. Certainly, I am talking about more than His personality and His knowledge. To quickly get to the point, I am talking about how Jesus did these works.

How did Jesus do what He did? Did Jesus do these things because He was God? If He did, then one of two things must be true, neither of which is acceptable. Either Jesus did not mean what He said, which you know is not the case. Or, we must be on the same level as Jesus as some type of deities. You know that is not the case.

Jesus told the men who traveled with Him they could do the things He did and greater things. He must have anticipated that these men could raise the dead, open blind eyes, walk on water, and slip away from danger when it was necessary. Somebody may read this far in my introduction and wonder why I am being so extreme.

My answer is simple. I believe. I am a believer and not a doubter. However, I see a huge problem, and I refuse to sit by and disappoint Jesus. I am committed to spending the rest of my life doing all I know to do, completing my assignment.

Many people have received the Holy Ghost and speak in tongues. A lot of them will even prophesy. This is wonderful. There should be even more people speaking in tongues and prophesying. But being filled with the Holy Ghost is much more than I just described.

It is about power. The things Jesus did require a power often missing in the church today. That power is coming back. We call it the Great Awakening. I don't want to give you the full answer in this introduction. I want you to read the book. I am confident I have discovered the answer to the mystery. If I tell you what it is without the proper setting (which is the life of Jesus), you will probably miss the most essential ingredient. You will need to read the book to find out what this is.

The Holy Spirit was deeply involved in shaping the life and ministry of the wonderful person we call Jesus. It all began before Jesus was born. The influence continued until the day He ascended back into heaven. This study will start to examine many of the things which Jesus said and did, specifically relating to the Holy Spirit. After all, Jesus did introduce the world to this awesome third person of the Godhead.

You will find six of the most well-known stories about the life of Jesus on the following pages. I will be doing more than repeating these stories. I have a plan, and I will be very open about it. I believe the Holy Ghost was always at work in the life of this man we call Jesus. He was unlike any other man before Him. There has been none exactly like Him since His return to heaven.

I am not taking this approach just because it was Jesus saying and doing these things. This would be reason enough. It certainly adds great significance and validity to the subject.

However, I am doing this because it will provide a firm foundation for anyone God uses in any area of ministry.

For years, I have had questions for which I have never found a sufficient answer in any of the books about the Holy Spirit. Neither have I heard these things addressed adequately in sermons and teachings. This has motivated me to seek the answers for myself directly from the Word of God.

This approach means you will find very few other authors quoted in the following pages. If you find what appears to be a quote with no reference attached, there is a reason. Either it was buried deep in my memory, and I have no idea where it came from because if I did, I certainly would give credit. Or, it means the Holy Spirit has shown someone else the same truth He has given to me, and I did not know it.

In this book, you will notice that, at times, I will use the words Holy Spirit. At other times, I will use the words Holy Ghost. They are the same. Some prefer one over the other. Many of the Bible translations use both and use them interchangeably. I will follow this pattern.

With that said, here is a list of questions to which you will find the answers in the pages of this book. The only way to find the correct answers is to ask the right questions. I believe these are the right questions.

As a man, how did Jesus relate to the Holy Spirit?

Was this only a divine relationship?

Was the relationship between Jesus and the Holy Ghost a human-to-divine relationship, much like ours?

What can we learn from Jesus about the guidance of the Holy Spirit? Did The Holy Spirit guide Him? Are there examples of this in the Bible?

Did Jesus say or do things that connect His earthly ministry to the operation of the gifts of the Holy Spirit? If so, where are they found? Which gifts were they?

We will look carefully at the impact of the Holy Spirit on the life of Jesus. You may be pleasantly surprised at what we can learn from what happened to Jesus because of the Holy Ghost.

It is truly a fantastic thing to know your purpose in life. This is mine. It is the study and the revelation of the Holy Spirit and His gifts. To God be all the glory for any revelation I have received.

Chapter 1
When Jesus Broke the Silence

When God came to Earth, no one was expecting Him. Heaven had been silent for hundreds of years. There was no indication at the temple that God was coming to earth. They thought they had everything under control. Each day the doctors of the law carried on with their mental gymnastics. The high priest continued his political maneuvers, and he certainly did not expect God to show up looking and acting like a man. No one expected anything this radical.

So that I don't confuse you, let me be clear. I believe Jesus was God who inhabited human flesh. This raises one of the most complex issues in Christianity. How could Jesus be both God and man? As many attempts as there have been, no one can explain this. Lay all that aside and shift your thoughts to what the angel Gabriel said to Mary. Try to imagine yourself in Mary's place. She was young, and nothing like this had ever happened. After you read the conversation between Mary and Gabriel, I challenge you to answer the questions I will raise.

> *Now in the sixth month the angel Gabriel was sent by God to a city of Galilee named Nazareth, to a virgin betrothed to a man whose name was Joseph, of the house*

7

of David. The virgin's name was Mary. And having come in, the angel said to her, "Rejoice, highly favored one, the Lord is with you; blessed are you among women!" But when she saw him, she was troubled at his saying, and considered what manner of greeting this was. Then the angel said to her, "Do not be afraid, Mary, for you have found favor with God. And behold, you will conceive in your womb and bring forth a Son, and shall call His name JESUS. He will be great, and will be called the Son of the Highest; and the Lord God will give Him the throne of His father David. And He will reign over the house of Jacob forever, and of His kingdom there will be no end." Then Mary said to the angel, "How can this be, since I do not know a man?" And the angel answered and said to her, "The Holy Spirit will come upon you, and the power of the Highest will overshadow you; therefore, also, that Holy One who is to be born will be called the Son of God. Now indeed, Elizabeth your relative has also conceived a son in her old age; and this is now the sixth month for her who was called barren. For with God nothing will be impossible." Then Mary said, "Behold the maidservant of the Lord! Let it be to me according to your word." And the angel departed from her. (Luke 1:26-38 – NKJV)

If the angel Gabriel said these things to you, would you conclude this baby would be a human child, or would He be God? Don't answer this question based on what we know today. Mary had no access to this information.

Base your answer on what you think Mary would have known. Mary did not understand the greeting. It bothered her to hear herself receive such accolades. What could Gabriel possibly mean by saying she was highly favored? She didn't know anyone else an angel had said that to. Why her?

Most of the great things Mary, the mother of Jesus, was told about the baby could have a natural meaning. This is true of *the throne of David*. And except for the word *forever*, this is true of what Gabriel said about *the house of Jacob*. The Jews expected God to deliver them by sending a natural man to restore the Nation of Israel. This was what they thought they wanted. Perhaps you recall this conversation.

> *Therefore, when they had come together, they asked Him, saying, "Lord, will You at this time restore the kingdom to Israel?" And He said to them, "It is not for you to know times or seasons which the Father has put in His own authority. (Acts 1:6-7 – NKJV)*

This question came from men who had spent three years with Jesus. They had heard all the things Jesus had said about His purpose in coming to earth. Many times, the disciples had heard Jesus explain that He was God. This was the resurrected Lord they were talking to. Yet, they still held out hope for Jesus to be an earthly king. If these men did not understand that Jesus was more than a man, how could Mary have understood?

Jesus was, and He is, the Son of God.

During His earthly ministry, Jesus often endeavored to make this clear. His greatest challenge was getting the people to believe He was the Son of God. Jesus came to bridge the gap between man and God.

He came to restore the relationship between man and God. Only a person who was both God and man could do this. It was the plan of the Father. It was the plan of redemption.

From the earliest moment in the life of Jesus, men have attempted to see Jesus as being only God or only man. He was both, and He still is both. What matters is the way we view His interaction with humanity. When Jesus healed the lame man, was He acting as God or man? Was Jesus doing something we can do? He said that He was.

I have often seen people struggle with the same problem the people of Israel had when they saw Jesus perform a miracle. They thought only God could do things like this. But Jesus was a man. On more than one occasion, they preferred to believe Jesus was a devil instead of believing in the power of the Holy Ghost. So, what I am going to do is take you on a journey through the first thirty years of the life of Jesus.

I want you to see Him as a man.
But not just any man.

When Jesus encountered people with leprosy, He healed them. Any other man would have kept his distance and insisted the lepers do the same. Jesus touched them.

It was a real human touch they received. However, it was a touch filled with power. Jesus was a man full of the Holy Ghost. We will not be doing any damage to His image as God. We can't. Jesus will still be the Son of God no matter what I say or write. However, I might be able to get those who read this book to believe they can do what Jesus did.

Most of the world is familiar with at least some version of the story of the birth of Jesus. It has been repeated for hundreds of years. Granted, to some people, it is only a story. And, interestingly enough, it is the part about the angels that really seems to ring a bell with a lot of people. I am primarily referring to their announcement of the birth of the baby Jesus. The story of the angels certainly provides us with a beautiful picture. Sadly, for many people, it is not much more than that.

On the night Jesus was born, extraordinary stories from the shepherds began to swirl through the community. The shepherds said angels appeared and announced that a Savior had been born. This did not seem right. Why would the Son of God show up as a baby? Israel needed a king to overthrow the Roman Empire. Somebody said this baby was the Son of God. How could this be? He cried. He had to be fed. He could not walk or talk. He could not even hold His head up. Does this sound like God? Was this really what the angel was talking about when he appeared to Mary and Joseph? Those shepherds did not make their story up to get attention. It happened just the way they told it. And it was an experience that none of them would ever forget.

As Gabriel explained to Mary how Jesus would be born, he mentioned how the Holy Ghost would be involved. The Holy Ghost came to this earth. Now understand that the Holy Ghost did not come to everybody. He only came to Mary to make sure Jesus was born. Maybe this is the best way to express it. Jesus did not come to earth alone. The Holy Spirit came with Him, and until Jesus was dying on the cross, the Holy Spirit never left Him for one second.

Gabriel told the Virgin Mary that God had chosen her to do what no other person has ever done. She would give birth without ever having been with a man. This was absolutely unheard of, and yet Mary accepted this and seems to have asked Gabriel no questions about the results. I find this to be remarkable. The mention of the Holy Spirit did not seem to alarm Mary.

I do not mean to imply that Mary understood these things. I don't believe she did. Those words spoken by Gabriel to Mary are exceedingly lofty. What did Mary know about the Holy Spirit? Why was she so willing to comply? We attribute this to great faith, and indeed it was. I am also thinking about the baby Jesus. *That Holy One who is to be born will be called the Son of God.* What a declaration! Could Mary have known this was God's only Son? If so, what did Mary think this meant? She had no idea He was going to be crucified. No one on earth understood the plan of God. These are things we know, but she could not have known. The Holy Ghost had to be here. He is the one who reveals the truth. Let's look once again at the words of the angel Gabriel.

> *"The Holy Spirit will come upon you, and the power of the Highest will overshadow you; therefore, also, that Holy One who is to be born will be called the Son of God." (Luke 1:35 – NKJV)*

This is amazing. Was this all the angel had to say?

How much did Mary understand about the average human process of giving birth to a baby? Mary was very young when all this happened. She may have known a lot. There were no hospitals like we have today. Most babies were born at home and so it is entirely possible that Mary had witnessed the birth of a baby. However, this was giving birth to the only God-man to ever live. What did this mean?

The birth of Jesus is so ensconced in Christmas tradition that it is easy to miss the profound nature of the event. The Holy Ghost was here to make sure Jesus was born to a young virgin. Very few people knew Mary and Joseph. They were not married. Joseph did not even know about all of these things at this particular time. A few hours later, an angel came to Joseph, and may I say, the angel told Joseph as much as he needed to know. And that is all!

The whole concept was not even in the imagination of any man or woman. It was shrouded in mystery. In the wisdom of God, there was a unique plan for Jesus to come to earth without any person or even hell being able to disrupt the plan. On the one hand, it all seems strange. Yet the birth of Jesus was so normal and ordinary that it could have been overlooked. This allowed the angels and the Holy Spirit to make sure the only people who knew what was happening were those who would be glad and believe. As you will see later, they maintained this atmosphere for about two years.

When we think of the Holy Spirit and His power, we often desire to see Him draw a lot of attention to what is taking place. Much of what the Holy Spirit does, happens in silence. He is very clandestine in His maneuvers. The Holy Spirit knows the power of surprise for our arch-enemy. All you need to see this is true is to look at the birth of Jesus. The simple words to this beautiful Christmas song say it so well.

Oh, little town of Bethlehem, how still we see thee lie. Above their deep and dreamless sleep, a silent star goes by. Yet in thy dark streets shineth, the everlasting light. The hopes and fears of all the years are met in thee tonight. For Christ is born of Mary and gathered all above. While mortals sleep, the angels keep their watch of wondering love. Oh, morning stars together, proclaim thy holy birth. And praises sing to God the king, and peace to men on earth.[2]

The more I think about this story, the more I admire this young lady. Her faith in her ability to know God spoke to her through this angel is astonishing, especially with so little information. Then, readily and fully embracing what was being told to her goes beyond a level of faith I have rarely seen.

The angel was describing to her how the Holy Spirit would work in her life to bring about the birth of the Lord Jesus. This was not something Mary had read about in a book as we have. To proceed with the direction given to her by the angel required a level of trust and obedience, which is remarkable. Think for a moment about what this says to us. Thankfully Mary was not as hesitant about obeying the Holy Spirit as most people seem to be today.

Because of Mary, the Holy Ghost was at work in the life of Jesus before He breathed His first breath of air on earth.

The first chapter of Luke's gospel provides an amazing record of the work of the Holy Spirit in the family into which Jesus was born. Elizabeth, Mary's cousin, was filled with the

Holy Ghost and prophesied. Zacharias, the husband of Elizabeth, was filled with the Holy Ghost and prophesied. Mary, the mother of Jesus, gave us the wonderful song of praise, commonly called the **Magnificat**.

These precious surroundings for the baby Jesus were vital for His time on earth. The Holy Ghost was at work creating the right atmosphere for Jesus when He was a child. The influence of the Holy Ghost in His life was profound.

When Jesus was approaching His last few minutes to be on the earth in visible form, He had a special meeting with some of His close followers. At the end of His time on this earth, it was Jesus who spoke about the work of the Holy Spirit in our lives. These are the words Jesus said to His disciples before He ascended back into heaven.

> *"But you shall receive power when the Holy Spirit has come upon you; and you shall be witnesses to Me in Jerusalem, and in all Judea and Samaria, and to the end of the earth." (Acts 1:8 – NKJV)*

The similarity of the language used by Jesus and the angel is striking. The Holy Spirit came upon Mary, and the Holy Spirit came upon these people Jesus spoke to that day.

A significant change came to Mary, and a significant change came to the people Jesus spoke to. This is one of the essential indications that one has received the Holy Spirit.

We expect people to change when they are born again. And thankfully, many of them do change. I have often wondered about those who appear to make no changes in their behavior.

It is not my place to judge anyone. But I can't help but wonder how anyone who experiences the new birth can stay the same.

It has been my experience that most Christians do not expect much change in the life of a person who receives the Holy Ghost. I think there should be remarkable changes after a person receives the Holy Ghost. The Holy Ghost comes to live in us forever. How could we not change?

These are valuable lessons we have learned from the story of the birth of the Lord Jesus. The Holy Spirit is deeply invested in what Jesus came to do. Over 2000 years later, the Holy Spirit is still following through on the plan. He evidently sees us as having great value in the kingdom of God.

As we continue to follow the life of Jesus, I believe you will agree that the Holy Spirit was involved in every facet of His life. **The Holy Ghost knows first-hand what it is like to see the life of God resident in human flesh.** He saw the first person this happened to. His name is Jesus. He is the God-man, both completely God and completely man living in human flesh. First, Jesus had a natural body; now, it is an eternal body. For all of eternity, *we shall be like Him because as He is so are we in this world.*

Chapter 2
He Woke Up in Egypt

Mary, Joseph, and Jesus made a trip to Egypt in the middle of the night according to Matthew's gospel. The first thing I find so interesting about this part of the story is that it is not recorded in any of the other Gospels. It surprises me that the other writers omitted this part of the story. It is filled with remarkable detail. In many ways, this journey in and out of Egypt is reminiscent of the Israelites' time in the same country. Both Joseph and his family and Jesus and His family were guided in and out of Egypt by the hand of God. In both cases, it was to preserve the plan of God. The first journey preserved the descendants of Abraham. The second journey preserved the Kingdom of God.

Under the Old Covenant, the angels were often assigned the task of communicating with man. The people under the Old Covenant were not born-again, meaning their human spirits were not alive unto God. The Holy Spirit did speak to certain extraordinary people to do things for God. But there are also people God used, and as New Testament believers, we may never understand why He chose them. We are left to wonder and marvel at the workings of God.

Always remember that God is not bound or limited in any way except as He has chosen to be.

Many miraculous stories do not fit what we know about how God does things. Jesus has appeared to some of the vilest people on earth. Men and women who knew almost nothing of God have been afforded visitations. With these thoughts in mind, I want to consider the following stories. It is all blended, yet several distinctly different things were going on.

> *Now after Jesus was born in Bethlehem of Judea in the days of Herod the king, behold, wise men from the East came to Jerusalem, saying, "Where is He who has been born King of the Jews? For we have seen His star in the East and have come to worship Him." When Herod the king heard this, he was troubled, and all Jerusalem with him. And when he had gathered all the chief priests and scribes of the people together, he inquired of them where the Christ was to be born. So they said to him, "In Bethlehem of Judea, for thus it is written by the prophet: But you, Bethlehem, in the land of Judah, are not the least among the rulers of Judah; For out of you shall come a Ruler who will shepherd My people Israel." Then Herod, when he had secretly called the wise men, determined from them what time the star appeared. And he sent them to Bethlehem and said, "Go and search carefully for the young Child, and when you have found Him, bring back word to me, that I may come and worship Him also." When they heard the king, they departed; and behold, the star which they had seen in the East went before them, till it came and stood over where the young Child was. When*

they saw the star, they rejoiced with exceedingly great joy. And when they had come into the house, they saw the young Child with Mary His mother, and fell down and worshiped Him. And when they had opened their treasures, they presented gifts to Him: gold, frankincense, and myrrh. Then, being divinely warned in a dream that they should not return to Herod, they departed for their own country another way. Now when they had departed, behold, an angel of the Lord appeared to Joseph in a dream, saying, "Arise, take the young Child and His mother, flee to Egypt, and stay there until I bring you word; for Herod will seek the young Child to destroy Him." When he arose, he took the young Child and His mother by night and departed for Egypt, and was there until the death of Herod, that it might be fulfilled which was spoken by the Lord through the prophet, saying, "Out of Egypt I called My Son." (Matthew 2:1-15 – NKJV)

It has always intrigued me that this group of men came from the east searching for a baby. There are theories about how these men knew about Jesus, but I don't know if any of them are correct. So, I won't repeat them. They did call Him *The King of the Jews*. Jesus came into the world with this accolade, and He was crucified with these same words nailed to the cross on which He died. When they arrived, the wise men spoke to several people and finally to Herod. The wise men shared why they had traveled such a long distance to reach Jerusalem. The very thought of another King of the Jews being born angered Herod so much that he made the effort to trick the wise men into helping him find baby Jesus.

Perhaps the fact that Herod's trickery failed is one of the reasons why we call these individuals wise men. When this attempt to fool these men failed, Herod was determined to kill Jesus, and many little boys lost their lives because of this evil man, Herod.

The wise men found Jesus and presented their various gifts to Him, and worshiped Him. It is at this point that I want to dive deeper into the story. I will begin with the ultimate horror that occurred (at least in part) because of the wise men's decision not to tell Herod where Jesus could be found. This horrible part of the story often causes it to be left out when the Christmas story is shared.

> *Then, being divinely warned in a dream that they should not return to Herod, they departed for their own country another way. (Matthew 2:12 – NKJV)*

It would be easy to skip over this detail and not pay much attention to what happened. This was an act of God. The best way to express this is to say the Holy Ghost was at work. The birth of Jesus occurred due to the combined work of the angels and the Holy Spirit. Once again, I conclude that it was this combined work of the angels and the Holy Spirit that kept these wise men from returning to Jerusalem.

I firmly believe this was not just three wise men traveling alone. Simple logic says otherwise. Travel in that part of the world was dangerous. This probably was a rather large party traveling together. It does not seem reasonable to think they could leave that area completely unnoticed. Yes, I am suggesting the Holy Ghost was involved in orchestrating this departure.

Herod was intent on finding Jesus so he could have Him killed.

My theory is that Herod had a large group of evil men available to him who were willing to do whatever vile thing he told them to do. They killed hundreds of little boys. These same men would have captured and perhaps even killed these wise men if they had caught them purposely defying the wishes of King Herod. The Holy Ghost was protecting Jesus. At the very least, it is safe to say the wise men could have been forced to divulge the whereabouts of the location of Mary, Joseph, and the young child Jesus.

What happened next is very intriguing. Jesus was two years old or less. No one knows for sure. Perhaps you noticed these words in the story. *And when they had come into the house, they saw the young Child with Mary His mother, and fell down and worshiped Him.* The family had moved out of the place where Jesus was born, and they were living in a house. This is one of the indications that time had passed from the birth of Jesus until the arrival of the wise men.

He is called a *young child* and not a baby.

Irrespective of the passing of time, Jesus was undoubtedly keeping the angels busy. You know, all of heaven was watching. Of course, I mean the heavenly Father, the Holy Spirit, and countless angels. There was no way the plan of God would be stopped or even disrupted.

When the wise men left, another angel appeared, and this is all we are told about this next significant event in the life of Jesus.

Now when they had departed, behold, an angel of the Lord appeared to Joseph in a dream, saying, "Arise, take the young Child and His mother, flee to Egypt, and stay there until I bring you word; for Herod will seek the young Child to destroy Him." When he arose, he took the young Child and His mother by night and departed for Egypt, and was there until the death of Herod, that it might be fulfilled which was spoken by the Lord through the prophet, saying, "Out of Egypt I called My Son." (Matthew 2:13-15 – NKJV)

The quote at the end of verse 15 of the above passage was taken from a prophecy which can be found in Hosea 11:1. What follows is a shift back to the information regarding the evil King Herod. Perhaps it is best to allow you just to read it.

Then Herod, when he saw that he was deceived by the wise men, was exceedingly angry; and he sent forth and put to death all the male children who were in Bethlehem and in all its districts, from two years old and under, according to the time which he had determined from the wise men. Then was fulfilled what was spoken by Jeremiah the prophet, saying: "A voice was heard in Ramah, Lamentation, weeping, and great mourning, Rachel weeping for her children, Refusing to be comforted, Because they are no more." Now when Herod was dead, behold, an angel of the Lord appeared in a dream to Joseph in Egypt, saying, "Arise, take the young Child and His mother, and go to the land of Israel, for those who sought the young Child's life are dead." Then he arose, took the young Child and His mother, and came into the land of Israel. But when he heard that Archelaus was reigning over Judea instead of his father Herod, he was afraid to go there. And being warned by God in a dream, he turned aside into the region of Galilee. And he came and dwelt in a city called Nazareth, that it might be fulfilled which was spoken by the prophets, "He shall be called a Nazarene." (Matthew 2:16-23 – NKJV)

These scriptures contain a prophecy from Jeremiah 31:15, which was fulfilled by the actions of King Herod. Since only Matthew records this part of the story of Jesus, it is logical to assume that Matthew felt an obligation to connect these events to the **fulfillment of these prophecies.**

Joseph had another visit from an angel who instructed him to take his family back to the land of Israel because the person who wanted to kill Jesus was dead. Joseph moved back to Israel. However, Archelaus, the son of King Herod, was now the king. The reaction from Joseph was fear. For the third time in this story, an angel appeared to Joseph and warned him of the impending danger. They did not return to Bethlehem, but instead traveled to Nazareth and made their home in that city. Another prophecy was fulfilled.

"He shall be called a Nazarene." ³

This story provides an example of a significant aspect of the nature of prophecy. Many people believe that all prophecies will automatically come to pass. This is not always the case.

Every part of this story required the decisions and the actions of the people involved for the prophecies to be

fulfilled. We are not robots void of a freewill. God respects and honors our choices, even when we are not doing what He wants us to do. Of course, we suffer the consequences of our disobedience. No doubt, the visits from the angels were compelling. We do not usually have such an experience because, as born-again individuals, in most cases, it should not be necessary for an angel to tell us what we should do.

This is a part of the purpose and the work of the Holy Ghost. Jesus told us this very clearly.

> *Howbeit when he, the Spirit of truth, is come, he will guide you into all truth: for he shall not speak of himself; but whatsoever he shall hear, that shall he speak: and he will shew you things to come. (John 16:13 – KJV)*

Both Joseph and these wise men experienced the work of the *Spirit of truth*. They were shown things by the Holy Ghost that would not have happened had they not done as the *Spirit of truth* told them to do. We must not only hear and receive information regarding the future, but we must also do something with it.

By looking at the fulfillment of these prophetic words about Jesus we can learn a great deal regarding how the Holy Spirit will work in our lives if we will just listen. It is not wrong to avoid danger. Do not get in the habit of immediately rebuking fear. Find out why you are afraid. Then listen for the Holy Spirit to instruct you. He stands ready to work in our lives and on our behalf, just as He did in the life of Jesus.

A little boy, who probably slept on the journey to Egypt, was protected by the Holy Spirit. He woke up safe and sound.

Chapter 3
The Family Business

Our study of the Holy Ghost in the life of Jesus continues with the account we are given of Jesus and His family taking another trip. This was a trip to Jerusalem. This story is not so much about what Jesus and the others said, instead it is an account of some of the things Jesus did. The detail of what happened shines an engaging, informative, and exciting light on our subject.

Luke begins his account of this story by explaining why the family made this trip to Jerusalem.

> *His parents went to Jerusalem every year at the Feast of the Passover. And when He was twelve years old, they went up to Jerusalem according to the custom of the feast. When they had finished the days, as they returned, the Boy Jesus lingered behind in Jerusalem. And Joseph and His mother did not know it; but supposing Him to have been in the company, they went a day's journey, and sought Him among their relatives and acquaintances. So when they did not find Him, they returned to Jerusalem, seeking Him. Now so it was that after three days they found Him in the temple, sitting in the midst of the*

teachers, both listening to them and asking them questions. And all who heard Him were astonished at His understanding and answers. So when they saw Him, they were amazed; and His mother said to Him, "Son, why have You done this to us? Look, Your father and I have sought You anxiously." And He said to them, "Why did you seek Me? Did you not know that I must be about My Father's business?" But they did not understand the statement which He spoke to them. Then He went down with them and came to Nazareth, and was subject to them, but His mother kept all these things in her heart. And Jesus increased in wisdom and stature, and in favor with God and men. (Luke 2:41-52 – NKJV)

Each time I read this story, it reminds me of a family who attended the church where I was the associate pastor in Fort Worth, Texas. I worked at this church while I was a seminary student at Texas Christian University.

This family had four young boys. Each Sunday, they would drive over an hour to come to our church. I am sure they got up very early to get to church in time for Sunday School. Getting four young boys ready for church can be an ordeal.

On several occasions, when the church service was over, and everybody had left, I would go through the church building, making sure all the lights had been turned off. It was not unusual for me to find one of these four boys lying under one of the church pews, sound asleep.

At first, the boy who did this quite often was scared when I woke him up, and he realized his parents had forgotten him.

It took over an hour for his parents to drive back to the church to pick him up. Little by little, he relaxed as he came to trust my wife, Donna, and me. He knew he was going to be safe. Nevertheless, this was a traumatic experience for him to realize he had been forgotten.

These were not bad parents. Preoccupied, yes, but good parents. They loved their kids. I know this to be a fact. Later on, this family moved to another state, and on one occasion I stayed in their home. We just decided to make a joke out of the whole ordeal, and the mom and dad became known among several of us at the church as Mary and Joseph. Everybody involved knew what we were talking about, and the teasing didn't bother them at all.

Isn't it interesting that the parents of the Lord Jesus did not go straight to the temple when they were looking for Him? I have to wonder why? If they had been thinking like Jesus, and I am saying had they thought the way He was thinking about Himself, the temple would have been their first destination. The fact they were not thinking this way says a lot about the way Jesus was growing up.

It is obvious that Mary and Joseph were not expecting Jesus to be in the temple. We can assume there was nothing about the temple that reminded them of what the angels had said about Jesus at the time of His birth. Considering how the leadership of the Jews treated Jesus a few years later, I believe this is a safe conclusion.

Jesus did not fit the mold of the person the Jewish leaders were expecting in a Messiah.

It appears Jesus spent almost an entire week in the temple without His parents. I am considering the time it took for them to walk back to the city and the days they spent looking for Him. According to the story we have, it appears Jesus was very content and happy to be there alone. Jesus showed no signs of anxiety or fear. In the heart and mind of Jesus, He was busy doing His Father's business.

At the very young age of twelve, Jesus was revealing He was not an average young boy. There was something different about Him. Jesus was very intelligent, but that is not my point. He proved He was astute when He was in the temple, however I am considering a deeper level. I want to draw your attention to the fact that He already knew a lot about spiritual things, and this is what motivated Him to be in the temple.

His interest in spiritual things made Him stand out. I do not view His questions to the doctors in the temple as a matter of arrogance. Instead, I view this as an example of His desire to be taught by those older and wiser than He was at this age. Jesus had a great desire to learn.

I propose that when Jesus went to see these men in the temple, He may have been seeking to learn in two distinctly different ways.

There were things Jesus wanted to know, which He thought or perhaps hoped these scholars might know. I also wonder if maybe He knew things at this tender age that no one else in His family or circle of friends seemed to know. He wanted to know if these men who were supposed to represent His Father knew these things. Wouldn't it be fascinating to know what these questions were?

Revelation is available at a very young age.

Jesus knew who His Father was. There appears to have never been any question about this. Joseph and Mary knew who His Father was. Yet, by the wording in the Scriptures I just quoted, it is clear their understanding of what this all meant was, at this point, minimal. When Jesus told them He needed to be about His Father's business, they did not seem to relate this to His relationship with God.

I suggest Jesus wanted to know if the doctors and the priests would know who He was. After all, this became a common issue in the ministry of Jesus. His claim regarding who He was caused the Jews to crucify Him. At least, it became their excuse.

Was Jesus already raising this issue at the age of twelve? I believe so. He did ask His parents the question. *Why did you seek Me? Did you not know that I must be about My Father's business?*

The *Easy-to-Read Version* of Scripture provides a very intriguing translation of these words of Jesus.

> *Jesus said to them, "Why did you have to look for me? You should have known that I must be where my Father's work is." (Luke 2:49 – ERV)*

If this translation is accurate, which these authors believe it to be, it gives some additional insight into the mind of Jesus at this young age. This causes me to wonder if this is more akin to what Jesus said to His parents. I am attempting to balance this with what I perceive to be a very mild-mannered and obedient young man. Did Jesus tell his parents they should have known He would be where His Father's work is?

If Jesus actually said, *You should have known that I must be where my Father's work is,"* this would certainly have afforded Mary and Joseph an opportunity for great conversations with Jesus. They would surely have identified this place *where my Father's work is* as the temple. Perhaps this thought has occurred to you. Jesus did not say He wanted to be **where His Father was working.** There is a great deal of difference between where a person is actually working and where their work is. The first refers to where the action is taking place. It is where something is happening. The second only speaks of a location. I wonder if Jesus realized after spending time in the temple, His Father was not working there. What a great disappointment that would have been!

Considering that Joseph, His natural father, was a carpenter, this concept of Jesus saying, *You should have known that I must be where my Father's work is,* does present an interesting situation. Joseph did not work in the temple. Surely this thought crossed Mary's mind and Joseph's as well. "Jesus must know more about who He really is than we have ever discussed."

The Bible does not reveal what Mary and Joseph had shared with Jesus about the miracle of His birth. I think, indeed, they must have told Him every detail. I would think they had done this many times. If we choose to look at His questions from this perspective, it opens up a fascinating view of what was already happening in the life of Jesus.

I have heard references made to this story in Luke, and remarks were made that indicate some view this as a bit of rebellion on the part of Jesus. These remarks by Jesus have been viewed as almost sarcastic or as a rebuke to His parents. I don't think this was the case. This was a 12-year-old boy on a mission He believed was right.

My view of Jesus as a young boy is that He was a loving and respectful son of His natural earthly parents. Because I think of Him in this way, I believe Jesus was expressing His surprise at the reaction of Mary and Joseph. Jesus anticipated they would expect Him to do what He had been doing. He wanted Mary and Joseph to embrace who He was fully.

It might seem I am imposing the actions of Jesus in His adult life on this event which happened when He was twelve. Perhaps I am. But I don't think so. It seems to be that Jesus was maturing rather quickly.

The word picture we are given of Jesus in the temple says to me that He had fully embraced His true identity as the Son of God. He was ready, at least for His parents, to be in this same place. However, the story implies this had not yet happened.

We can conclude that Jesus had been in the temple for about five days when His parents found Him. We don't know how much of this time He spent talking to these doctors. Who were these "doctors" mentioned in this story?

The Greek word for **doctors** used in this story references the teachers of the Jewish religion.[4] I find it interesting that at such an early age, Jesus chose to engage the very people in conversation who would later oppose Him so viciously. I am not suggesting Jesus knew of this.

I take this to be an outstanding example
of the grace of God.

The appearance of Jesus with these Jewish religious leaders causes me to have many questions. Perhaps the most important question is why didn't they seem to remember Jesus a few years later when He was a grown man? Why didn't this at least cause some of them to wonder about His true identity?

Of course, to some degree, we have the same uncertainty about the identity of Jesus with His natural parents. The angels had told them who He was. Maybe the real problem can be found in their lack of understanding of His real purpose. Why was Jesus born? What did *save His people from their sins* mean? It certainly means a lot to us because we understand salvation by grace.

In all fairness, we must keep in mind that the parents of Jesus were devout Jews. Until this point in their lives, they had a very structured relationship with God based on the Law of Moses. Only the priest dealt with sin. The high priest covered the people's sins once every year by offering to God an animal sacrifice. Nothing about Jesus fit this pattern. These thoughts certainly give meaning to the words of the apostle Paul.

> *For what the law could not do in that it was weak through the flesh, God did by sending His own Son in the likeness of sinful flesh, on account of sin: He condemned sin in the flesh. (Romans 8:3 – NKJV)*

When Jesus walked this earth, Jesus was just as human as you and I are. I realize this may be hard to imagine, but it is true. He was also the Son of God. The amazing thing is that

Jesus is still a human. He just has a body that is very different from the kind of body that we have.

No, I can't explain how this can all be true. No one can. The Biblical record and the historical evidence are proof enough to satisfy me.

For a moment, let's take another look at this passage from Luke's gospel.

> *Now so it was that after three days they found Him in the temple, sitting in the midst of the teachers, both listening to them and asking them questions. And all who heard Him were astonished at His understanding and answers. (Luke 2:46-47 – NKJV)*

Three things stand out to me in those verses. Perhaps it strikes you in the same manner.

The first of these is the boldness found in Jesus. Most adults would never be this bold. They would have been intimidated by this group of men. These were highly educated men who had a lot of power and authority. Jesus appears to have been very respectful but, indeed, not fearful.

If the timing of this event has been a question in your mind this can be resolved by the fact that Jesus was safe because He was a child. He could be very bold and not be in danger. These men would protect a child and see that no harm came to Him.

Jesus not only asked questions of these doctors, but Jesus could also answer their questions. The third thing that strikes me is the understanding Jesus had at this point in His life.

Where or from whom did Jesus learn all of these things? Did Mary and Joseph teach him? Were His parents this knowledgeable of spiritual things? If so, then these people were not just poor, ignorant people, as some scholars might like for you to believe.

If Mary and Joseph were not the sources of the knowledge Jesus shared with these men in the temple, there were at least two other possibilities. First of all, Jesus had been able to spend a lot of time with other people in the area where He was growing up who knew a lot about spiritual things. No doubt, Jesus spent time with Elizabeth and Zacharias. They were much older than Mary and Joseph, so we don't know how long they lived after their son John was born. Perhaps Zacharias had taken Jesus to the temple several times with him. We have no proof of this. However, it does provide exciting reflection.

The other source of this knowledge could have come to Jesus directly from His heavenly Father. It is entirely possible, and I would say even probable, that the heavenly Father had begun revealing things to Jesus at a very early age. If this is confusing to you, keep in mind that Jesus was dealing with His human intellect. He needed to be taught. He needed to learn and to grow. I don't just mean the growth of His human body. This is borne out in this same passage.

If nothing else, Jesus was curious about the level of spiritual understanding these religious leaders had. He was listening intently to what the doctors had to say. He was engaged in conversation and discussion with them. They had to be intrigued by this bright young man.

We are left to wonder if these Jewish leaders remembered this time in the temple later as they heard Him speak. Did it ever cross their minds that this was the same young man who had spent several days with them? I think we can be sure Jesus was quoting things they had said to Him.

He remembered them!

As I have indicated, nothing in the story ever seems to imply Jesus was rude or arrogant. He was just asking questions and answering questions.

I have always wondered if Jesus asked them a question they could not answer. If He did, I would sure like to know what the question was. I am not thinking of the typical kid-type question for which there is no answer. Did He raise a question they had asked each other? The story does not mention this. We will never know.

It fascinates me that Mary and Joseph appear to be as amazed by Jesus and what He did in the temple as the religious leaders were. On the one hand, this surprises me. Yet, at the same time, it reveals how normal these people really were. It is for these reasons I don't think they had taught Him all of the spiritual things He knew. I believe the Holy Ghost was at work revealing many wonderful things to the young Jesus.

We must take a closer look at the following verses. The last verse answers some of the questions I have just raised. And it validates several of my previous statements about Jesus.

So when they saw Him, they were amazed; and His mother said to Him, "Son, why have You done this to

35

us? Look, Your father and I have sought You anxiously." And He said to them, "Why did you seek Me? Did you not know that I must be about My Father's business?" But they did not understand the statement which He spoke to them. (Luke 2:48-50 – NKJV)

No matter what we may think of how the translators have handled these statements, one thing comes through clearly. Jesus was surprised His parents were looking for Him. Jesus believed He was doing what He was supposed to be doing.

I will not take the time to veer off my subject to cite specific examples. However, a little meditation on this issue will remind you of numerous times in the life and ministry of Jesus when He was doing what He was supposed to do. Yet, those around Him did not recognize this fact. Again and again, Jesus seemed surprised that His people (the Jews) could not or did not understand His purpose and mission.

Then again, perhaps it was more a matter of Him expressing disappointment than it was an expression of surprise. Perhaps the wording in the translations could be better.

I must raise these questions. Are we often guilty of the same thing? How well do we understand the real purpose of Jesus' coming to earth? Sure, we know He came to die for our sins. Thank God He did. However, Jesus also came to introduce the world to the third person of the Godhead. I am speaking of the magnificent Holy Spirit.

From a very early age, Jesus knew much about who He was and why He was here on this earth. Everything we know about what He did and said was intended to fulfill His purpose. How did He know to do these things?

It intrigues me that the young boy Jesus knew He needed to interact with the Jewish leaders in the temple. He knew He needed to learn things from them. They knew natural things Jesus probably did not know. I take my clue about these statements from the fact that He acted on His desire to be with them and talk to them. What caused Him to be so drawn to the temple?

I come back to the same question again and again. Why was it so hard for Mary and Joseph to understand these things? Every time I consider the story of Jesus from when Mary and Joseph first knew about the baby, to the grand announcement of Jesus' birth in the stable, I am in awe. When I consider the record we have, it causes me to want to assume a particular attitude would exist in Mary and Joseph, which the Biblical narrative does not seem to verify. Would I have been more aware? I seriously doubt it.

I would not be surprised if the story said Jesus' parents took Him to the temple and left Him there for three days. This would be what I would have expected of them. It didn't happen that way. Evidently God did not expect this of them.

Having such an ordinary boy for a son, might have dulled the anticipation of these parents for anything out of the ordinary in His actions. Yet, at the same time, I must admit some of this had changed by the time He reached the age of thirty. Mary, the mother of Jesus, did expect Jesus to be able to do something about the lack of wine at the wedding. There had to be some reason Mary thought Jesus could do something about the lack of wine. She must have seen changes in Him that were fascinating. This could very well be indicated in the words of this verse from our story.

Then He went down with them and came to Nazareth, and was subject to them, but His mother kept all these things in her heart. (Luke 2:51 – NKJV)

Perhaps you remember Mary did a very similar thing after the shepherds had come from the fields to see the baby Jesus. The shepherds left the place where Jesus was born, and they told everyone who would listen about the great things that had happened the night the angels appeared to them.

The people were wondering about this great news. No doubt, the word spread quickly because it was such an extraordinary story. Yet, we have this reaction from Mary.

But Mary kept all these things and pondered them in her heart. (Luke 2:19 – NKJV)

Chapter 4
Wisdom, Maturity, and Favor

By the time Jesus was ready to begin His ministry, the Holy Spirit had been at work in His life for about thirty years. We don't know all the details, but as you have seen in reading the previous chapters of this book, it is clear that the Holy Spirit was with Jesus and was teaching Him on a very regular basis. It also seems obvious that Mary, the mother of Jesus, had seen something about Jesus, which caused her to believe Jesus could do something about the shortage of wine at a wedding they attended.

From what little information we have, Jesus was a normal young man. By normal, I mean He does not appear to have lived as a monk or done strange things as He was growing up. He had friends. He seems to have worked alongside of His earthly father and learned many things from him. There is no doubt He had chores to do and was taught to be a responsible young man. All of this is made evident by these words from the writer of the book of Hebrews.

> *For we do not have a High Priest who cannot sympathize with our weaknesses, but was in all points tempted as we are, yet without sin. (Hebrews 4:15 – NKJV)*

Statements in the Bible such as those more than imply how much Jesus the man, was like us. The verse is stated in the negative, but it is saying how much Jesus identified with what we experience. The verse also makes it clear that temptation is not a sin. Jesus was tempted. But Jesus never sinned.

Despite all we know from the revelation given to us in Scripture, it appears Mary and Joseph may have spent the early years of Jesus' life never expecting anything out of the ordinary from Him. Because we have the opportunity to look back on who Jesus became and what He did for us, this seems remarkable. When we look through the lens of our understanding, we imagine a very different young man. We may be inclined to think surely Jesus healed people He encountered when He was a teenager.

Relying totally on the information given to us in the Scriptures, we know this did not happen. There was much preparation made for the ministry Jesus had on this earth, and it all began at the right time.

Spiritual things are normal. The Holy Spirit is normal. Some Christians seem to feel otherwise as they seek for extraordinary spiritual experiences. I have often wondered if those I have just described understand the danger involved in their desires. The weirdness in this world happens outside the realm of the Spirit. Never should we mix the two.

My favorite part of the passage we are studying is perhaps this verse.

> *And Jesus increased in wisdom and stature, and in favor with God and men. (Luke 2:52 – NKJV)*

If Jesus needed to increase in this way – then so do we. It may be amazing to think of Jesus requiring more wisdom, maturity, and favor with God. But it must have been so. When I consider this, my thoughts immediately turn to those who hated Him so much that they killed Him. It may be easy to think that if Jesus had only used a little more wisdom, surely, He could have gained a little more favor with the religious leaders and not suffered the crucifixion. This was not the plan of God. Jesus was not lacking in wisdom. The lack was on the part of those who hated Him.

Without a doubt, Jesus needed wisdom, maturity and favor as He spoke to the vast crowds who gathered to hear Him teach. As Jesus moved among the throngs of people that were healed by Him, a level of maturity and knowledge of what to do and how to do it was necessary.

Jesus was doing things no one had ever done!

Thousands of people we know nothing about were healed when they got close to Jesus. These people may not have been present to defend Him when the angry mob took steps to crucify Him. Yet we cannot deny He left an impact on their lives. Many of them probably became a part of the first church formed after Pentecost. Their relatives and the generations that followed had considerable influence on what transpired as the church of the Lord Jesus developed and grew.

The Holy Spirit was at work in the life of Jesus. This was true before He reached the age of twelve. And although we are not given any further detail, the Holy Spirit continued to be at work in His life as an adult.

From what we know about the child Jesus, we can rightly conclude that many kids can learn and understand spiritual things. This understanding may happen at or perhaps even on a deeper level than many adults experience. The church should be taking more advantage of this opportunity. This is not intended as an insult. Instead, it is meant to be informative.

Many churches have missed this great opportunity in their approach to providing ministry to children. If what is taking place in the adult service is as it should be, then perhaps it would be healthier (from a spiritual perspective) for the children to spend more time in the adult service seated next to their parents. If this were to take place, we might have better kids, better families, better churches and a better nation.

I understand it takes a lot of work and effort to keep kids interested in the things in life that are important. Much of their time is spent being entertained. But what is offered to the kids at church should not just be entertainment. It must be full of substance and spiritual significance. When this does not happen, the church is not fulfilling its commission and purpose.

It is my firm belief that church should be something we all enjoy. It should never be boring. I have said many times I think going to church should be fun. At no time am I referring to foolishness when I make such statements. Neither am I talking about comedy and entertainment, just for the sake of making people laugh. Some things are just naturally funny. God does funny things. The Holy Spirit will cause people to do funny things.

However, when church for any age group mainly focuses on entertainment, it has veered off course. Sadly, this often seems to be the primary criteria for a lot of what is offered today to adults and kids. These things do not ever create spiritual growth and maturity. Our job is much too significant, especially when it comes to our children, for us to be satisfied with knowing our kids had a good time at church, and we never stop to find out why. Was it because they got to play their favorite video games at church?

There are three things that are very important in every person's life. These three things are essential for us to do what God put us on this earth to do. We can never fulfill the purpose for which we were born without these three things.

Just as it happened in the life of Jesus, we all must grow in wisdom, stature, and favor. The great corporations of the world spend a lot of time, money, and effort to develop and increase these three things in natural ways in their employees. Sadly, the church puts very little effort into producing the same results on a spiritual level.

I see these three different character traits illustrated in the life of Jesus. It is clear to me that this is one of the fundamental reasons we have this story about Jesus in the temple as a 12-year-old boy. It is remarkable how much wisdom Jesus demonstrated at such a young age. Something about Jesus garnered great favor with the doctors in the temple. The Holy Spirit was doing His part.

The best time for developing these three things is when a child is very young. Without doubt this is the plan of God for every child.

The Holy Spirit stands ready to do his part. The rest is up to us.

Please consider what I have said in light of this statement made by Jesus during the days of His ministry.

> *Let the little children come to Me, and do not forbid them;*
> *for of such is the kingdom of heaven.*
> *(Matthew 19:14 – NKJV)*

Jesus was very keen on the matter of reaching the children.

Children have great favor with God. The stories abound to back this up. You may have one or more of your own. I certainly do. Rest assured, even when they are grown and have their own families, these adults can and should continue to grow in favor with God. The growth of our favor with God will also cause our favor with the right people to grow. They may not be the people we want to have favor with at that moment. Yet, they will become the right people as God's plan for our life unfolds. Many people have failed to recognize this and have paid dearly because of it. The fact that God has great plans for us is precisely the reason why God will give us favor with certain people. These may be people we don't even like.

Interestingly enough, our actions and words often determine the growth of our favor with people. It is our wisdom, or the lack thereof, which determines our words and our actions.

Think of it this way. God will give us favor where we need it most. Our wisdom and maturity will determine whether or not we keep and benefit from the favor God has given to us. Indeed, there is much more involved. For example, other people can get involved in these relationships and, for a time, disrupt the favor God has given us. Nonetheless, we should do our best to do our part. And if we do the right thing, God will ultimately turn things around for us. I have seen it happen many times.

Kindness pays great dividends.

When I think back over my life, there is only one explanation for why I have been able to go where I have gone and do what I have done. There is only one reason why I have been associated on a personal level with some of the spiritual giants of my lifetime. It can all be attributed to the favor of God.

Remember, no limit has been set on the amount of wisdom, maturity, and favor you can have. All of these can keep growing as long as you live on this earth. It is also essential to never separate these three things, because the moment these three things (wisdom, maturity, and favor) are separated in a person's life, the growth of all three will stop. Why is this true?

These three aspects of our lives are mutually dependent on each other. Wisdom requires maturity. Favor involves maturity. However, without having favor with wise people, none of us can mature. What benefit is wisdom if you have no favor in your life which allows you to use it? What good is maturity if you lack wisdom? What benefit are you to someone who will show you favor if you lack wisdom and maturity? I think you see my point.

We can quickly damage or even destroy
the favor given to us by God,
by not using wisdom and by not having maturity.

Many parents have made a colossal mistake and thought their little kids were not interested in spiritual things. When children are small, getting them saved and filled with the Holy Ghost is easy. They are very interested because sin has not tainted and distorted their lives. Their attention span may be relatively short. I do understand that. They have no interest in staying focused on an hour-long message. I know this too. I have watched any number of kids grow restless while I was preaching. However, you might be surprised at how much they hear when they do not appear to be listening. Never draw the conclusion that the Holy Spirit is not at work in your children. He is there all the time.

When both of our boys were young, we set up a ministry tour involving about six churches stretching from Ohio and Pennsylvania to North Carolina. The whole trip took almost a month of their summer. So, we scheduled stops at various theme parks along the way. We were traveling in a custom van equipped with a cassette tape deck.

At the time, cassette tapes were the latest and best way to listen to music and teaching tapes of various singers and ministers. I had purchased a set of cassette tapes from Pastor John Osteen of Houston, Texas. He was one of my favorite speakers. The man had a real gift of communication. The title of the series of messages was, *Living in the Super Supernatural.*

We drove one day for several hours and stopped to eat lunch before continuing to our destination for that particular day. As we drove, we listened to these tapes by Pastor John Osteen. Our two boys had been playing in the back of the van.

After lunch, we got back in the van, and we did not turn the tape player back on. My wife and I thought a few minutes of quiet so we could talk was a good idea. After about 45 minutes, one of our boys asked us to play some more of the tapes by Pastor Osteen. We did, but we wondered why they were so interested. Pastor Osteen was a great speaker, but these were kids!

Later on, we figured out the story Pastor John told about his wife Dodie believing God for a swimming pool, had gotten their attention. We also found out they wanted to know more about how this worked. How do I know this? Because those two boys figured it out and began praying for God to give us a house with a swimming pool. It was not very long until we got a house with a pool. Do I believe God answered the prayers of two young boys? Yes, I do.

Never discount the spiritual things children can learn and receive from listening to adults at church. This is true in both a negative sense and a positive sense. I certainly hope the church catches on to the positive side of this.

We are living in a very messed up world. It seems that only weird things and perverse things are considered normal. I would be willing to guess that the study of abnormal psychology today is all about what was once thought to be common sense. This is because social norms are what this field of study uses to define normal. I don't need to tell you there are many strange things that some people desire to be accepted as normal. I never dreamed we would live in a world like we see every day. So many people have no concept of normal. It is a tough time to be raising children. It is a tough time to be alive on planet Earth.

I am ultimately writing about the Holy Spirit, with particular emphasis on what Jesus taught on the subject. At the same time, it is essential to reinforce the fundamental basis for which we must consider things to be normal in our minds. There still is a real normal.

We tend to think of natural things as the litmus test for normal. As we move deeper into the Great Awakening, it will be evident that this assessment is completely wrong. It is only spiritual things that are normal. We are spirit beings. We have a soul (a mind) and live in a physical body. With only a moment of thought, you know which of these is more important to the ungodly. It is the body.

You and your children are spirit beings. The Holy Spirit is at work in all of your lives. This is true whether you and your children are born-again or not. The real difference is what the Holy Spirit is working on in each life.

The Holy Spirit is just as active in all of our lives as He was in the life of Jesus.

Then He went down with them and came to Nazareth, and was subject to them, but His mother kept all these things in her heart. And Jesus increased in wisdom and stature, and in favor with God and men.
(Luke 2:51-52 – NKJV)

I have shared several things regarding wisdom, stature (or maturity), and favor with God and man. It is important to add that the foundation of it all is good parenting. This is one of the most significant problems we have in America today. Too many kids have no father in the home! Also, an increasing number do not have a mother either.

Jesus was never a rebellious child or teenager. Besides myself, I know of many others who can say the same thing. Rebellion is not normal behavior. It always has a root cause. At times, this rebellion is the result of parents not doing the job God has assigned to them as parents. They either don't know how to do the job or want someone else to do it for them. There can be other causes of rebellion, such as the wrong influences in their lives. Schools are incapable of parenting. Yet, many school boards keep insisting on greater control. This must be stopped.

Sadly, we are dealing with something in our society which has been developing for several generations. Occasionally, a person who becomes an adult without the aid of good parents recognizes the source of their problems and sets out to correct them. People such as this can and often do become good parents. They have learned both the need for it and the value of it. They learned it the hard way.

Keep this in mind and keep it in your heart as you pray for the Great Awakening. This awakening must have a profound impact on the families of our nation.

I anticipate that many mothers will read this book and like Mary, the mother of Jesus, they will be reminded of things they have kept in their hearts. I encourage you to believe that as long as your children are alive on this earth, it is never too late for God to do a great work in their lives. Keep believing and keep praying for the Holy Spirit to touch the heart of your child or children, as the case may be. He is ready and willing.

Stay strong and never give up.

By now, I am sure you know why I find this to be such a remarkable story about the life of Jesus. As I have expressed in these few pages, it becomes authentic when we look at His family. Hopefully, it has become something you can connect with to help you in your life. This is my purpose for writing this book.

As strange as this may sound to you, Jesus grew into the person He needed to be. You and I can do the same. Our children and our grandchildren can do the same. Nothing about this world can stop us unless we allow it. Just don't allow it!

You may wonder how you are to do such a thing. Here are a few thoughts to help you. God has already given each of us favor with Him regarding salvation. The Scriptures about this are very clear. This favor with God can and will grow as our spiritual maturity, and willingness to obey the voice of the Holy Spirit grows.

Every time the Spirit of God speaks to you and you obey, you grow. Every time the Spirit of God speaks to you and you obey, you grow. Every time the Spirit of God speaks to you and you obey, you grow. Every time you follow the leading of the Holy Spirit, you grow spiritually. **I encourage you to read that paragraph several more times.**

This is not difficult to understand. We all know there have been small things the Holy Spirit instructed us to do, and we did not do them. This does not mean it is too late. Start today.

You may know many people who never do anything God tells them to do. You certainly don't have to join that crowd. Walk and live in harmony with God even if the rest of your family does not. You may be the actual source of change in your family. I do not mean your words. I am talking about your actions.

I am only trying to make this as straightforward as possible. If the Holy Spirit tells you to leave a tip for a waitress who has done a terrible job, would you do it? Maybe it is only five dollars. The person does not deserve it. You may want to talk to the manager and get the person fired. It would be more beneficial to follow the direction of the Holy Ghost. Life in the Spirit is this real and this down-to-earth.

Our actions always determine whether or not our favor with God and man will grow. This is not a matter of being legalistic. It is simply the way things work in life.

Favor will put you where you need to be in life. Wisdom and maturity will keep you there.

I believe the Holy Spirit drew Jesus to the temple for this extraordinary time in His life to help Him grow. Jesus had excellent parents. Yet, the Holy Spirit knew Jesus would not learn from His parents everything He needed to learn in order to do what He was sent to earth to do.

This is a clear message to every parent and grandparent to make sure their children and grandchildren have every opportunity to experience spiritual things for themselves on a mature adult level. They need to see the Holy Spirit working in other mature adults they respect.

The churches I attended as a child did not have a kid's church for me to go to. I grew up attending the adult service. Because of this, I got to know my pastor, and as a little boy, my pastor became my friend. Sure, I got in trouble for talking too much in church. What kid hasn't? Sure, at times, I got bored. What kid hasn't?

Yet, something genuine was happening inside of me. I saw adults worshiping God with all their hearts. None of them were perfect. But I observed their efforts to live their Christian lives. This was an essential part of my spiritual growth.

I received the Holy Spirit and spoke in tongues for the first time when I was 12 years old. This did not make me a perfect teenager. I am not sure there is any such thing as a perfect teenager. However, I saw adults who knew more about God than I did. I wanted what they had. This was especially true of my pastors. I had three different pastors from age four until I was eighteen. These men were not perfect and I knew it.

I saw one of them greatly mistreated by people in the church. I saw anger. Then I saw maturity. I watched God bless one of these men as he went on and followed God's leading in his personal life. In so many ways, these men are why I have spent my entire adult life in the ministry. I can only hope I have had a similar influence.

I will end this chapter with a short story about one of my pastors. He hired me to work for him the summer after I graduated from high school. This pastor was also a home builder. I was hired to do menial jobs for the great salary of fifty cents an hour.

I had driven our old family car several times, but I did not know how to drive. My pastor bought a brand-new Ford pickup truck. He had only owned it a few days when he drove to the job site where I worked for him. He tossed his keys to me and said, "Take my truck and go pick up some sand." My pastor looked at me and said, "You can drive, can't you?" I told him I did not have my driver's license. He responded, "You don't have far to go; just be careful." He walked away, and I drove off in his brand-new truck. I remember thinking how cool this was. It did something on the inside of me. I was very careful with my pastor's truck. I made sure nothing bad happened to that truck.

As you might have guessed, I drove that truck for the rest of the summer. Now for the purpose of the story. I had favor with this man. He saw maturity in me, which I did not see in myself at the time. I can't say this was the wisest thing my pastor ever did, at least as far as his truck was concerned.

Yet, on the other hand, it was an awesome sage thing. He demonstrated trust and confidence in me, which profoundly impacted my life. We all need someone to believe in us, even at a minor level. Pastor Warner believed in me. He never said it. I just knew it.

This increased my ability to believe in myself.

I enrolled in a local college and studied to be an architect. That is what my natural mind wanted to be. My spirit was saying otherwise. I did draw a complete set of house plans for one of the custom houses my pastor built. But he was never more pleased than he was when I told him I was going to Bible College to be a preacher.

I saw the Holy Ghost at work in all three of my pastors. At the time, as I was growing up, I did not know enough to say this. However, I knew there was something about them that I wanted. I saw the Holy Ghost at work in them. This is the crucial part. Maturity, wisdom, and favor tend to breed these same things in other people.

If you wonder how this can be true, I will simplify it. The desire born from seeing first-hand the benefits of a life lived in favor, maturity, and wisdom fuels this same desire and fire in others. God give us more of this in our society and especially in our churches.

Chapter 5
Baptized Like a Sinner

It would be fascinating to have more detail about the daily life of Jesus from the time of His birth until the beginning of His earthly ministry. However, the objective in the plan of God is not for us to just believe in a man who was like us. Instead, our commandment is to believe in the risen Jesus and call Him our Lord and Savior. He must always hold this significant place in our hearts. Jesus must unequivocally be the Master of your life and mine. This is the only way to salvation. Nothing less will do.

As I began writing about the six great events that shaped the life of Jesus, I saw an important pattern develop. It had nothing to do with His age. Rather it seemed to be all about touching different people groups. There were shepherds and other very ordinary individuals. Next came the wicked King Herod, who had many little boys killed. At the same time, other powerful men worshiped Jesus. In a matter of months, the Son of God had touched people from the Far East to the land of Egypt. Jesus was still very young, but already the One who came to set the captives free had traveled to the very place where His people had been in bondage for hundreds of years.

Because of what we know about the rest of the story of Jesus, the days Jesus spent in the temple with another group of people seem to be the most amazing. God gave these people a wonderful opportunity to get acquainted with His Son. What a powerful illustration of the following words.

> *For God so loved the world, that he gave his only begotten*
> *Son, that whosoever believeth in him should not perish,*
> *but have everlasting life. (John 3:16 – KJV)*

Salvation, as we know it was not yet available. But believing in Jesus certainly was! The shepherds believed. The Wise Men believed. King Herod did not believe. There is no record of the people in Egypt believing this. The intrigue of the Doctors of law in the temple did not count for everlasting life. They proved it later.

When Jesus became an adult, there was one special man God had prepared who believed in God's only Son. His name was John, and God had given him a significant assignment. We often only connect this man to the water baptisms he regularly performed. Yet his mission was much greater than the water he used. It was greater than the clothes he wore and the kind of food he ate.

John was preaching repentance to the sinners Jesus came to save. The prophet Isaiah had spoken these words about John hundreds of years before his ministry began.

> *The voice of him that crieth in the wilderness, Prepare ye*
> *the way of the LORD, make straight in the desert a*
> *highway for our God. Every valley shall be exalted, and*
> *every mountain and hill shall be made low: and the*

crooked shall be made straight, and the rough places
plain: And the glory of the LORD shall be revealed, and
all flesh shall see it together: for the mouth of the LORD
hath spoken it. (Isaiah 40:3-5 – KJV)

What a thrill it would have been to hear John preach. Apparently, he was rough in appearance and even in his speech. But undoubtedly, he was a man with a tender heart. Men and women with hard hearts do not care about the lost.

Jesus knew who John was. He knew about his preaching. Isn't it interesting how the Holy Spirit was shaping and molding the life of our Lord? From my past studies, I have seen very little attention given to how these events may have impacted the life of Jesus. Considering this to be also true of His ministry, it is essential to look at how the Holy Spirit was at work using these times to teach Jesus and prepare Him for what He would face.

Never forget that Jesus was human. He had feelings and emotions just like us. Maturity can only come with time and experience. Wisdom must be tested. Encounters with those who love you and those who don't are essential to our development. So it was with Jesus.

The fourth epic event in the life of Jesus is the story of His water baptism. It seems remarkable for Jesus to have even considered this to be necessary. Yet, He did. And it may have been much more significant than many have assumed.

There are three versions of the story of the water baptism of Jesus. They are recorded in the gospels of Matthew, Luke, and John. It is important to look at all three to draw specific comparisons. Combining the three stories provides a more complete picture of what happened on that particular day. I will begin with the story as Matthew tells it in his Gospel.

> *When He had been baptized, Jesus came up immediately from the water; and behold, the heavens were opened to Him, and He saw the Spirit of God descending like a dove and alighting upon Him. And suddenly a voice came from heaven, saying, "This is My beloved Son, in whom I am well pleased." (Matthew 3:16-17 – NKJV)*

In this story as it appears in the book of Luke, you will notice a detail missing from the account given by Matthew.

> *When all the people were baptized, it came to pass that Jesus also was baptized; and while He prayed, the heaven was opened. And the Holy Spirit descended in bodily form like a dove upon Him, and a voice came from heaven which said, "You are My beloved Son; in You I am well pleased." (Luke 3:21-22 – NKJV)*

Luke begins his account of this great event by letting us know Jesus waited until after all the other people had been baptized before He entered the water. This act alone speaks loudly of the nature of Jesus. His entire life was about putting others first. This was humility. There is no question about that. Actually, it was much more.

The Holy Ghost was at work in the heart of Jesus. He knew He had not come to earth for Himself. He came for us. It may not seem like much on the surface for Jesus to wait until the others had been baptized, unless you consider that Jesus was always making an important point in all He said and did.

Jesus never wasted an opportunity.

Jesus always made it clear when speaking to His disciples that He was the Son of God. He was obvious and purposeful in demonstrating that He was the son of man. Presenting Himself as both was part of the plan.

Now let's examine what John adds to this story.

> *And John bore witness, saying, I saw the Spirit descending from heaven like a dove, and He remained upon Him. I did not know Him, but He who sent me to baptize with water said to me, Upon whom you see the Spirit descending, and remaining on Him, this is He who baptizes with the Holy Spirit. (John 1:32-33 – NKJV)*

Here is a list of some of the distinguishing characteristics of this event from each of these three writers. You will now get a better idea of what I intended by the comment earlier about a more complete picture.

Matthew says these things happened as Jesus was coming up out of the water.

Matthew and Luke both record that the heavens were opened.

None of the three explains what it means for the heavens to be opened.

John says in his account that John the Baptist *saw the Spirit descending from heaven.*

All three of these authors mention some type of creature that had the appearance of a dove. All three are very careful not to call this being a dove. There is nothing on earth in all of God's marvelous creations which can equate to the Holy Ghost. Yet, it is common to see a religious symbol of the Holy Spirit, and it is a dove. His attributes are much too complex for Him to be a dove.

The Holy Spirit is definitely not a dove.

It might be that this dove-like creature indicates peace and love. Perhaps God wanted to introduce the Holy Ghost to the world in a manner not previously thought of by the people of that time. There is no question in my mind that the dove-like creature represented the third person of the Godhead.

The message God the Father was sending about His relationship with Jesus was clear. No symbolism was necessary to help explain what the Father thought of His Son. We can glean the best understanding of this part of the baptism of Jesus through God the Father's own words He spoke from Heaven.

Months later, Jesus gave these instructions to the twelve disciples as He sent them out to minister. He made an interesting comparison between certain animals.

> *Behold, I send you out as sheep in the midst of wolves. Therefore be wise as serpents and harmless as doves. (Matthew 10:16 – NKJV)*

So that I do not distort any of the concepts Jesus was conveying when He made the statements I have just mentioned, I will only use the words He used to explain this. Then I will take these thoughts back to the story of His baptism.

In these statements, Jesus mentioned four creatures. He spoke of sheep, wolves, serpents, and doves. These four creatures were divided into two pairs in juxtaposition with each other. The idea was to help His disciples compare sheep to wolves and to make it more forceful to compare serpents to doves. What conclusions can we draw from this?

I have not spent as much time around sheep and doves as I have with horses, cows, cats, and dogs. Thus, I am drawing my opinions about sheep from comments I have read from former sheep owners. I can't properly document these comments because I do not know enough about these people to do so. But here is a synopsis of what they said. I found these comments on an online bulletin board called Quora.[5] This is not intended as an endorsement of this site.

The consensus is sheep are social, kind, and in some ways, serious and business-like. Every day they wake, eat, rest, move to other fields, eat and rest. It appears they will end the day where they started unless someone keeps them from doing so. If one of the animals finds something good to eat, they will announce it so all the rest of the sheep can share what they have discovered.

As a flock, they tend to circulate, so every animal has time on the outside edge and in the middle. I assume this is a way they share the risk of danger. Sheep have only one way to protect themselves. That is to run.

Several comments I read indicated that sheep are happy animals, especially when they are young. They can be seen running and jumping and playing games. Even as adults, sheep can be seen running and jumping if they have reason to be happy. I suppose the reason to be happy would have much to do with their surroundings, especially the humans with whom they must deal regularly.

What I just wrote provides great insight. First, this is how Jesus wanted His disciples (and us) to be: social, kind, and, when necessary serious and business-like. When He sent His disciples out, they were to take care of each other, see that each one's needs were met, and ensure they were all safe. I think, most of all, Jesus wanted His disciples to be happy. Jesus still wants that.

> *Therefore, do not let your good be spoken of as evil; for the kingdom of God is not eating and drinking, but righteousness and peace and joy in the Holy Spirit. (Romans 14:16-17 – NKJV)*

The happiest people in the world should be those who are filled with the Holy Spirit!

Consider the Holy Spirit in this same light. The Holy Spirit is very social. The Holy Spirit can be found in every nation without regard to race or color. He will fill and empower anyone who will receive Him. He is kind. He is generous. The Holy Ghost will protect us. He never leaves us alone.

By contrast, nothing about the Spirit of God should remind us of a wolf or a serpent. Thinking about this part could help us avoid many problems. If you encounter a wolf or serpent and don't have something to protect yourself, the results will not be good. Wolves and serpents hurt people. Something about their nature causes them to be this way. The Holy Spirit has none of this in His character.

Several years ago, there was a huge meeting in Tulsa, Oklahoma, with thousands of people in attendance. The central figure of the event is the most important part of this story and not the innocent people she chose to take advantage of the night this happened.

A lot of advertising and expense had gone into making the event possible. I chose not to attend. One of the speakers invited to this event was a lady who claimed to experience stigmata or signs of blood in her hands, forehead, and back.

Long ago, the prophet Isaiah clearly expressed who bled and died for us, and He still bears these marks on His body. Nothing in Scripture indicates this is something we can share.

> *Surely, He has borne our griefs and carried our sorrows; yet we esteemed Him stricken, smitten by God, and afflicted. But He was wounded for our transgressions, He was bruised for our iniquities; The chastisement for our peace was upon Him, and by His stripes we are healed. (Isaiah 53:4-5 – NKJV)*

This is a description of what Jesus suffered for us. Claiming to carry the wounds placed on Jesus is arrogant and offensive.

To make matters worse, this lady proceeded to scatter feathers on the stage and behind the piano in front of the audience. She was careful with this deception but not careful enough. She was caught on camera as one of the men behind the camera zoomed in on the lady and exposed her as a fraud. I saw the video, as did hundreds of other ministers. The feathers that the woman dropped on the floor were examined, and it was determined they were goose feathers from a pillow.

This happened many years ago. You might wonder why I am making mention of it in this book. I will be very clear.

I have never met this lady. Everything I know about her comes from what I have read, heard, or seen in the video I mentioned or what others have told me who knew her. I knew several people who were associated with this lady. So, why bring it up?

I chose to speak about this for two reasons. First, I was shocked that some of the people who knew this person were completely deceived. This level of deception is dangerous, and as the Great Awakening grows, the devil will be very busy with many different forms of deception. Secondly, this is a prime example of what Jesus warned against. I am referring to the wolves and snakes. This charade made a lot of money because the crowds of people who flocked to see her were huge.

This has nothing to do with the Holy Spirit that I know!

Now let's consider the dove aspect of the story. It was not a dove that came from Heaven, but it was a creature that was like the form of a dove. What else can we say about doves to give us more insight into the Holy Spirit? Once again, I will turn to the Internet.

One person said doves are not the kind of birds you can forcefully handle. They are described as rather delicate and easy to terrify. At first, I did not consider this helpful. Then I thought about it for a few minutes. You do not push your way around with the Holy Ghost. He is not the least bit afraid, far from it. However, I can assure you from many hours of experience that the Holy Ghost will withdraw when men and women start trying to make things happen. You may have heard the comment, "The anointing has lifted," or some similar statement. Invariably this means something displeased the Holy Ghost. Never forget, the Holy Spirit is always in charge, or He is not involved.

In a sense, this also seems to be true of a dove. The nature of a dove essentially puts the dove in charge of his life. Similarly, the Holy Spirit is always in charge because of His nature. The Holy Spirit does not typically do things by force. Because of His nature He does not need to use force.

Doves are very vocal birds. Most of the time, it is a soft cooing sound they make. Yet, at other times they can be very loud and relentless.[6] If you are filled with the Holy Ghost, then you already know this sounds so very much like the Holy Ghost. It is also how Jesus wanted His disciples to act.

The apostle Peter was often caught saying things when he should have been quiet. Undoubtedly, he embarrassed himself more than once. It took some time for Peter to learn when to speak and when not to. I suggest that Peter's words probably originated in a conversation with the Lord Jesus.

> *But sanctify the Lord God in your hearts, and always be ready to give a defense to everyone who asks you a reason for the hope that is in you, with meekness and fear; having a good conscience, that when they defame you as evildoers, those who revile your good conduct in Christ may be ashamed. For it is better, if it is the will of God, to suffer for doing good than for doing evil.*
> *(1 Peter 3:15-17 – NKJV)*

The Holy Spirit always has something to say. He is not a mindless chatterbox. It is just that the Holy Spirit knows everything that is happening around us. His nature is to protect us. He always has something helpful and encouraging to say. Most of the time His voice is soft but easy to hear and understand. If the Holy Ghost speaks loudly it is usually because we are in danger and not listening well or we need to take some immediate action. We all need to learn to listen more and to talk less. It seems the writer James understood this very well.

> *Understand this, my dear brothers and sisters: You must all be quick to listen, slow to speak, and slow to get angry. (James 1:19 – NLT)*

Chapter 6
I Saw the Spirit

From the discussion of this dove-like creature, the narrative of the baptism of Jesus quickly transitions to a deeper meaning of what transpired. In their accounts of the water baptism of Jesus, Matthew and John declare this creature was a *Spirit*. To precisely quote the record in John's gospel, he said, *I saw the Spirit descending from heaven like a dove.*

The man named John, who wrote the book that bears his name, does not claim to have seen this incredible sight. This John, the author of the book, is quoting what John the Baptist said about Jesus.

Consider the significance of this claim. *I saw the Spirit descending from heaven like a dove.* Regardless of what we conclude about a dove, claiming you saw the Spirit is remarkable. Why do I think this is remarkable? Because the common opinion is that *the Spirit* can't be seen. He is not visible to the human eye. He does not have a bodily shape of any sort.

I have only repeated the common wisdom on the subject of the visibility of the Spirit. I am not saying it is or it is not correct.

Obviously, He can make Himself visible.

When Luke speaks of this same part of the event, he declares that *the Holy Ghost descended.* If we combine the statements of all three sources, we must conclude that the Holy Ghost attended the water baptism of Jesus. He was present in some type of visible form. We can also conclude that the Holy Ghost looked nothing like a man. He had a very different bodily shape.

Perhaps this was the whole purpose of this dove-like creature. God wanted to distinguish between the human being Jesus exhibited Himself to be and the non-human nature of the Holy Ghost. This does not take away from what I have shared previously about the nature of a dove. It becomes more important.

Think about this part of the story in a different light. The people already had many ideas about God the Father. Some were correct, and some were very far from the truth. These same people were forming opinions about the Son of God. Yet, I believe it is accurate to say most of them had no clear ideas regarding the nature of the Holy Ghost.

Some of these people knew there was a powerful side to God, which you did not want to upset. They probably would have called this part of God's nature the Holy Ghost. In their history, the Jews had witnessed what could happen if God was made to be angry. Maybe this comprised their entire opinion of the Holy Ghost. My point is that the Jewish people at this baptism could have had a great fear of God and especially the Holy Ghost. They had heard the story about the earth opening up and swallowing people. If this does not sound familiar, here is the record of this event.

A group of wicked men stirred up a great controversy among the people of Israel. They attempted to usurp the authority God had invested in Moses and Aaron. One of their claims was that every person was holy, and Moses had no right to the place he held in the eyes of the people. This was an attempt at a coup. This group intended to overthrow the leadership of Israel. A man by the name of Korah was the leader of the group. After Moses spoke to God about this group, the results were astounding.

> *And Moses said: "By this you shall know that the LORD has sent me to do all these works, for I have not done them of my own will. If these men die naturally like all men, or if they are visited by the common fate of all men, then the LORD has not sent me. But if the LORD creates a new thing, and the earth opens its mouth and swallows them up with all that belongs to them, and they go down alive into the pit, then you will understand that these men have rejected the LORD." Now it came to pass, as he finished speaking all these words, that the ground split apart under them, and the earth opened its mouth and swallowed them up, with their households and all the men with Korah, with all their goods. So they and all those with them went down alive into the pit; the earth closed over them, and they perished from among the assembly. Then all Israel who were around them fled at their cry, for they said, 'Lest the earth swallow us up also!' (Numbers 16:28-34 – NKJV)*

There were probably people at the baptism of Jesus who could tell this story in great detail. You can see why it was important for God to introduce the Holy Ghost in a different manner. Jesus was going to be talking about the *Spirit*. Having a completely different frame of reference was necessary. The people who saw these things only had limited knowledge of God. He was a God of law and judgment. The concept of a loving heavenly Father and a covenant of grace and mercy was not a part of their mindset. Things were changing. And God was going to show it clearly from Heaven.

What happened next was the most extraordinary part of the baptism. A voice spoke from Heaven. How many times in the history of the earth has this happened? Not many, I am sure. I have never seen anything like this, but I would love to. It had to be amazing. No doubt it sent a chill up the spine of some of those people. Can you even imagine what this was like?

Apparently, they all heard God's voice! Only Matthew and Luke mention the voice. For some reason, this does not appear in the gospel of John. I wonder why.

In Matthew's account, the voice from Heaven spoke directly to the crowd. God said, *"This is my beloved son in whom I am well pleased."*

Luke's account differs significantly. God said, *"Thou art my beloved son; in thee I am well pleased."* The Father was speaking directly to Jesus. Apparently, the people heard this voice and this statement as well. Yes, I am saying I believe both accounts occurred.

The book of Revelation refers to many different types of creatures. Some of these descriptions do not fit anything we have seen on this earth. This does not mean the descriptions are false or misleading. I am confident that what John saw probably looked exactly as he described in his writings. However, I want to give you something else to consider.

After the opening comments of the book of Revelation, John makes a fascinating statement. It is one I have thought about many times.

> *I was in the Spirit on the Lord's Day, and I heard behind me a loud voice like a trumpet saying, "Write what you see in a book and send it to the seven churches, to Ephesus and to Smyrna and to Pergamum and to Thyatira and to Sardis and to Philadelphia and to Laodicea."*
> *(Revelation 1:10-11 – ESV)*

I know what it is like to be *in the Spirit on the Lord's Day*, or on any other day for that matter. It is not an easy thing to describe. We have nothing with which to compare it.

To be in the Spirit means your entire being is engulfed by the realm in which only the things of the Spirit of God matter.

I realize this may seem a bit strange to some who read this. It is wonderful. The details of your life, whether they are good, bad, wonderful, horrible, devastating, or exhilarating, are entirely irrelevant. If they are natural things, they are of no consequence.

The apostle Paul described his experience in this way.

> *I know a man in Christ who was caught up into the third heaven 14 years ago. Whether he was in the body or out of the body, I don't know, God knows. (2 Corinthians 12:2 – HCSB)*

No doubt, Paul was talking about himself and his experience when he wrote, *I know a man in Christ.* Why Paul chose to speak about this in the third person is something I have never resolved to my satisfaction.

An experience like this is impossible to explain. If it happens to you, be very glad. It will be a great experience but you will have a tough time explaining what happened to you.

If you are in the Spirit, you become unaware, oblivious if you prefer, to the world around you. Only what is happening to you because of the Spirit of God matters to you. It may even be funny or entertaining to people who observe this.

My point is simple. It is hard to explain the experience of being in the Spirit. So, you can imagine how difficult it could be to explain what you see and hear. We have nothing in the everyday world to use as a comparison.

When I take this a step further and remind you of what lies ahead, my purpose for bringing this up will become very clear. The prophet Joel gave us considerable insight into what will happen in the days to come.

> *And afterward I will pour out My Spirit upon all flesh; and your sons and your daughters shall prophesy, your old men shall dream dreams, your young men shall see visions. (Joel 2:28 – AMPC)*

Reading this one verse of Scripture could give a person the impression that the Great Awakening coming on the earth will only affect the men. Of course, this is not correct. The same verse states that this will impact *all flesh*. It is as if the Holy Spirit wanted to clarify this point because He continued with these words.

> *Even upon the menservants and upon the maidservants in those days will I pour out My Spirit. And I will show signs and wonders in the heavens, and on the earth, blood and fire and columns of smoke. (Joel 2:29-30 – AMPC)*

Every person who reads this book could very well be one of those people Joel spoke about in his prophecy many years ago. Not only will the Holy Spirit be poured out upon you, but you may also be one of those who is prophesying or having dreams and seeing visions. You may see signs, wonders, and unprecedented changes in the heavens and earth. You may have never been in the Spirit, and you may have never seen the Spirit. But if you are alive on this earth when these things take place, there is a huge chance you will spend considerable time in the Spirit.

You may tell a friend you saw something incredible but discover you are completely at a loss for words to describe what you saw. This brings me to a crucial question.

How prepared are you for the Great Awakening?

At the moment, it may seem as though I have completely left my subject. I haven't. This is a book about the Holy Spirit in the life of Jesus. All these things that happened to Jesus have a lasting impact on our lives as well.

73

Going right back to the story of the water baptism of Jesus, we discover another fact about the Holy Ghost. This information is given to us by both Matthew and John. It is the combination of their two statements that makes this exciting.

Matthew said those present on the day Jesus was baptized *saw the Spirit of God descending like a dove and coming to rest on him. (Matthew 3:16 – ESV)*

This is a remarkable statement. Watching this creature descend from Heaven and hover above Jesus when He came out of the water would have been exciting. But that did not happen. This dove-like creature came to *rest* on Jesus. John enriches the story a great deal more with his account.

> *And John bore witness: "I saw the Spirit descend from heaven like a dove, and it remained on him. I myself did not know him, but he who sent me to baptize with water said to me, 'He on whom you see the Spirit descend and remain, this is he who baptizes with the Holy Spirit.' "* (John 1:32-33 – ESV)

This is terrific. God gave John the Baptist a revelation regarding the coming of the Holy Ghost. It was then expressed in the words of John the Baptist and in a visual demonstration of what Jesus would talk about later when He spoke about the Holy Ghost.

Powerful messages were illustrated on the day Jesus was baptized in water. It is much too easy to conclude that teaching can only happen when the teacher says or writes something. Nothing could be further from the truth. What we have been given in this story about Jesus is a great example.

Jesus taught us a great deal about the Holy Ghost through His very actions. It was sometime later when Jesus uttered these words to the disciples.

> *"And I will pray the Father, and he shall give you another Comforter, that he may abide with you forever; Even the Spirit of truth; whom the world cannot receive, because it seeth him not, neither knoweth him: but ye know him; for he dwelleth with you, and shall be in you."* (John 14:16-17 – KJV)

I have no doubt this was the message Jesus wanted to communicate to those who watched His baptism. Jesus was not a sinner. The Bible makes this very clear. So then, why be baptized? Jesus did not need the remission of sins. He had none. No, Jesus had another purpose in being baptized. It was to identify with us. It was to show us that we need to be cleansed from our sins.

However, I ask you to consider another possibility. There may have been an even greater reason for this water baptismal service. It was not just to show Jesus being obedient in some way or being submissive. It was not just to give recognition or more validity to the ministry of John the Baptist. There was something else going on.

Jesus was demonstrating what can happen in the life of a person who has been freed from sin. The Holy Spirit of God will come to be with a person God has set free. And like this dove-like creature, the Holy Ghost will come to stay forever.

Did Jesus know all this would happen before He went to see John? We do not know. The Bible does not tell us the answer. However, we can say with certainty that the Father knew all this would take place, and so did the Holy Ghost. They may have told Him. Then again, Jesus may have just been following the leading of the Holy Spirit. I prefer to think it was the latter. Why?

I prefer to think Jesus was following the leading of the Holy Ghost because this is one more thing Jesus was teaching us that day. Wonderful things happen when we listen to the voice of the Holy Ghost. Exciting and meaningful things happen when we follow the leading of the Holy Ghost.

There is one more thought to consider regarding the water baptism of the Lord Jesus. Surely by now, you can understand why I have referred to this as an epic event.

I cannot just brush aside what John the Baptist said about this dove-like creature, especially what he said about how it behaved. It has much more to do with Jesus than with the dove-like creature.

> ...*He who sent me to baptize with water said to me, Upon whom you see the Spirit descending, and remaining on Him, this is He who baptizes with the Holy Spirit. (John 1:33 – NKJV)*

John the Baptist had been given an obvious sign and absolute instructions regarding the person who would baptize people with the Holy Spirit. No prophet had baptized people with the Holy Spirit, and neither had the priests or the kings. Such a thought had probably never occurred to them. The reason should be apparent. None of them were capable of such an act. Jesus was capable, and He still is.

What a moment this must have been for John. It must have been thrilling for him to have a word like this from God and see it happen in such a dramatic fashion. Jesus is the baptizer. Now there was no question, no uncertainty. John knew it for sure. Because what God had told John had come to pass. John saw the Spirit descending and remaining on Jesus. This was exceedingly important, not just for John but also for Jesus. What was going to happen to Jesus and through Jesus in the months ahead would require the ever-present power and ability of the Holy Ghost.

I am especially intrigued by the fact that the Holy Spirit *remained* on Jesus. This was something new. Jesus was the first person to have the Holy Spirit come to Him and never leave Him. This did not happen under the Old Covenant. In fact, we have these words recorded about King Saul.

> *Then Samuel took the horn of oil, and anointed him in the midst of his brethren: and the Spirit of the LORD came upon David from that day forward. So Samuel rose up, and went to Ramah. But the Spirit of the LORD departed from Saul, and an evil spirit from the LORD troubled him. (1 Samuel 16:13-14 – KJV)*

I am certain you noticed that *the Spirit of the LORD departed from Saul.* That much is clear. Of course, we know the reason the Spirit left him. It was not because of something that was a peculiar issue with the Spirit. The issue was with Saul and his disobedience to God. Some may want to argue that the Spirit would leave a person under the same circumstance today. I do not necessarily agree. We live under a covenant of grace not a covenant based on the Law. But these are issues to be discussed at another time. My purpose in choosing this scripture is the reference to David in contrast to Saul.

The Scripture says: *and the Spirit of the LORD came upon David from that day forward.* The Hebrew word for **came** is the word for **rush.**[7] I do not think this is understood as well as it needs to be. What we have in these words is an excellent example of the way a lot of people seem to think the Spirit operates today.

Strong compares this **rush** to a rushing fire. A fire burns itself out and then must be rekindled. This is how the Holy Spirit functioned with man under the Old Covenant. To make this clearer, think about what happens when accelerant like charcoal lighter fluid or gasoline is applied to a fire that is already burning. For a few minutes the flame gets hotter.

The flame is harder to control. The results are temporary and in the case of my example this is a good thing. This was not necessarily so when it came to the things of the Spirit. But the Spirit did not live and abide in man at that time.

The story of Samson is an excellent example of this **rush** of the Spirit. Here is one example.

> *And Samson called unto the LORD, and said, O Lord God, remember me, I pray thee, and strengthen me, I pray thee, only this once, O God, that I may be at once avenged of the Philistines for my two eyes. And Samson took hold of the two middle pillars upon which the house stood, and on which it was borne up, of the one with his right hand, and of the other with his left. And Samson said, Let me die with the Philistines. And he bowed himself with all*

his might; and the house fell upon the lords, and upon all the people that were therein. So the dead which he slew at his death were more than they which he slew in his life. (Judges 16:28-30 – KJV)

This story does not use the Hebrew word for **rush** and I do not mean to imply that it does. What I am attempting to convey is this concept of the Holy Spirit not being resident in the people of that time.

There is no better Scripture to explain the interaction between man and the Holy Spirit under the New Covenant than these words.

What? know ye not that your body is the temple of the Holy Ghost which is in you, which ye have of God, and ye are not your own? (1 Corinthians 6:19 – KJV)

Jesus promised that when the Holy Spirit came to earth, He would never leave us. He also promised the Holy Spirit would abide in us. He has kept this promise.

The Holy Ghost was just as important in the life of Jesus as He is in our lives. At this early moment in the ministry of Jesus, this was another lesson Jesus was teaching us.

We know the source of the baptism of the Holy Ghost. Another person of the Godhead has come to earth to stay with us. He is not only with us He is in us. He is not only in us we are in Him. Allow this to form in you great confidence regarding the Holy Ghost. Jesus taught us several notable things about the Holy Ghost by being baptized in water. This is not the place to stop in our understanding. It is the place to begin.

In the following chapters, I will discuss two more very important events in the life of Jesus. You will notice the focus in these stories slowly but clearly changes from Jesus to all of us who believe in Him. The events I have discussed thus far were mainly for His benefit and preparation. I want it to be clear that our personal benefit comes from our identification with Jesus and our observation of His methods.

What comes next will define the methods Jesus modeled for us.

These are not just casual words. It appears Jesus went straight from this glorious baptism into a confrontation with the devil. Some time may have passed, but it does not appear this way in Scripture.

It is very important how we view what took place during the time that Jesus spent in the wilderness. I have a firm belief that we have not handled this well.

The account of the wilderness temptation has been used to teach many things. I am asking different questions. What does this experience of Jesus in conflict with the devil have to do with us? Specifically, what was Jesus teaching us about the Holy Ghost when He spent time with the devil?

I will discuss how vital it is to be baptized in the Holy Ghost. Once again, Jesus will demonstrate what this means as we navigate through this world system under the dominion of the evil one.

Whatever you do, read these next few chapters very carefully. Then reread them. There is so much here from which you can benefit. In the next chapter I will begin to write about a familiar story that has often been distorted. Then we will look at some of the most amazing statements Jesus made during His ministry. This can be of tremendous help to anyone who will receive it.

Chapter 7
Led or Driven?

We will now take an in-depth look at what is commonly called the wilderness temptation, or as many have said, "the temptation of Jesus" in the wilderness. From my title to this chapter, it should be evident that I want to take a fresh look at what we are told in this very important story. To begin this part of our study I will admit that I question even the manner in which this story has been presented by the translators.

When the baptism of Jesus had ended, it appears this was the next thing to happen to Jesus. The Biblical authors made no real effort to present the story of Jesus chronologically, so we can't be dogmatic about this. However, most Biblical scholars seem to agree that this would have happened at or just before the beginning of the ministry of Jesus.

This opinion seems to be based on the words we find in the gospel of Luke. The translators of the *New King James Version* of the Bible make this point.

> *Now Jesus Himself began His ministry at about thirty years of age, being (as was supposed) the son of Joseph, the son of Heli. (Luke 3:23 – NKJV)*

If I had not italicized the entire verse, you would see the words, *His ministry at* were inserted in the *New King James Version*. The italicized words indicate that they were not a part of the original text.

I have included five translations of this same verse representing a wide span of theological perspectives. All of them except the *King James Version* say that this was the beginning of the ministry of Jesus. This indicates how strongly this opinion is held.

> *And Jesus himself began to be about thirty years of age, being (as was supposed) the son of Joseph, which was the son of Heli. (Luke 3:23 – KJV)*

> *As He began His ministry, Jesus was about 30 years old and was thought to be the son of Joseph, son of Heli. (Luke 3:23 – HCSB)*

> *Jesus was about thirty years old when he began his public ministry. Jesus was known as the son of Joseph. Joseph was the son of Heli. (Luke 3:23 – NLT)*

> *Now Jesus himself was about thirty years old when he began his ministry. He was the son, so it was thought, of Joseph, the son of Heli. (Luke 3:23 – NIV)*

> *The Genealogy of Jesus.[a] When Jesus began his ministry, he was about thirty years old. He was the son, as it was thought, of Joseph,[b] the son of Heli.[8] (Luke 3:23 – NCB)*

The *New Catholic Bible* is the last one quoted. I have included the footnotes at the back of this book. This is not an endorsement of the opinions stated. I have not discovered the source of the conclusions drawn by the author of these notes. I am only illustrating the level of research devoted to this topic.

As you can see, the opinions about the age of Jesus at the beginning of His ministry are widespread and very strong. The question is, does it matter? If the age of Jesus at the onset of His ministry does matter, then why? I believe I can answer these questions in very simple but accurate terms.

This is the only mention we have of the age of Jesus after the age of twelve. Perhaps this is to give us some level of confirmation of the statement made in the story of Jesus spending time in the temple. You will recall it ends with this declaration.

And Jesus grew in wisdom and stature, and in favor with God and man. (Luke 2:52 – NIV)

Having been the source of this information would be reason enough for Luke to include the age of Jesus with regard to the beginning of His ministry. Luke also makes another significant point in this same verse.

Perhaps you noticed the words *as was supposed* or *was thought to be the son of Joseph.* Then this is followed by the statement that Joseph was the *son of Heli.* You may also have noticed in your study of the Scriptures that this differs from what is found in the book of Matthew. Matthew has listed Jacob as the father of Joseph. If you glance back at the second footnote (found in my endnotes) from the *New Catholic Bible,* you will find an explanation of the difference between these two Gospels.

I have one other thought to leave with you before moving to the next part of this story. The Bible provides no information about the 18 years that transpired between when Jesus was in the temple and when He began His ministry. We can assume age is not an important factor to the Holy Spirit. What does matter is wisdom, knowledge, and understanding. Maturity is essential. It doesn't always come with age.

Maturity is the by-product of spiritual growth.

Earlier, I mentioned the lack of chronological order regarding the ministry of Jesus. I have a specific reason for desiring this. It is how the record of the wilderness temptation begins. John does not include this event in his gospel, so we will only look at the other three Gospels.

> *Then was Jesus led up of the Spirit into the wilderness to be tempted of the devil. (Matthew 4:1 – KJV)*

> *And immediately the spirit driveth him into the wilderness. And he was there in the wilderness forty days, tempted of Satan; and was with the wild beasts; and the angels ministered unto him. (Mark 1:12-13 – KJV)*

> *And Jesus being full of the Holy Ghost returned from Jordan, and was led by the Spirit into the wilderness, (Luke 4:1 – KJV)*

Each author begins this story with a conjunction. Mark adds the word *immediately*, which seems to be one of his favorite words. He uses it often. More importantly, using the conjunctions caused me to take another look at where the previous chapters had ended.

Matthew had just closed out his record of the story of the baptism of Jesus. His statement is the verse listed above.

Mark closed out his record of the water baptism in verse 11, just before the statement I have included above.

Luke placed the genealogy between his record of the water baptism and this story of the wilderness temptation.

I am not attempting to develop an argument for the chronological aspect of these stories. There is something else I find to be much more critical. I do believe Luke has captured this in the best way. It is a powerful teaching moment as we face our greatest enemy. I am referring to his use of these words, *And Jesus being full of the Holy Ghost returned from Jordan.*

What I find so important about this is the need to be full of the Holy Ghost when confronted with the devil's temptation. This is always essential no matter who you are. I do not mean to imply that others have overlooked or missed something. This is not the way I approach my understanding of the Gospels. I prefer to consider these differences as enhancements of those who have not recorded a particular detail. I will return to this matter at the end of this chapter and have more to say about it.

Now consider this significant difference between the wording in Matthew and Luke as opposed to what Mark has given to us.

Matthew and Luke stated that Jesus was *led up of the Spirit* or was *led by the Spirit*. These are very similar statements. I am emphasizing the word **led**. On the other hand, Mark uses an entirely different way of expressing what happened to Jesus.

87

Mark's words are these. *And immediately the spirit driveth him into the wilderness.*

I have chosen to use the old *King James Version* thus far because it is still the one many of my readers will have read. Let me highlight one other significant detail before discussing the words *led* and *driveth*. Understanding this difference is exceedingly important.

When you look back at the Scriptures from Matthew and Luke listed above, you will notice that the word *Spirit* is capitalized. In Mark's gospel, the word **spirit** begins with a small letter "**s**." The translators of the old version of the *King James Bible* wanted to distinguish between these two spirits. The first refers to the Spirit of God, or in context, to the Holy Ghost. The **spirit** spoken of by Mark is not the Holy Ghost. At least this would be true if there is validity to the word spirit not beginning with a capital letter. Some readers might think this is much ado about nothing. It isn't. Many people place a lot of confidence in things such as this. I will state my point in another fashion.

The Holy Ghost leads.
The other spirit drives or forces.

Occasionally, the choice of an English word in a translation inserts shades of meaning, distorting what was meant in the original language. I believe this is the case with the word *driveth*. So that King James English does not hamper us, I will provide another translation.

> *Immediately the Spirit [a]drove Him into the wilderness.*
> *(Mark 1:12 – NKJV)*

Before going further, we should take note of two things from this translation. The translators placed a footnote indicator next to the word *drove*. The footnote contains the phrase, *sent Him out*. The difference in the meaning of the words **drove** and **sent** is significant. Coupled with this, the translators chose to capitalize the word *Spirit*, indicating they had concluded this Biblical writer was writing about the Holy Ghost. This is not as tricky as it may seem. I intend to make it very clear. Because what you understand from this will profoundly impact how you view your dealings with the Holy Ghost.

Many other translations have very similar wording to the *New King James Version*. They also use the word *drove* and capitalize the word, *Spirit*. However, others read as follows:

> *At once the Spirit sent him out into the wilderness,*
> *(Mark 1:12 – NIV)*

In my opinion, this is a much better choice of words. I do not embrace the notion of the Holy Spirit driving Jesus or anyone else to do something. In my mind, the word **drive means to force**. The Holy Ghost does not force people to do things. Let's examine the meaning of these words in the Greek language.

The Greek word for **drove** means to lead one forth or away with a force he cannot resist.[9] It appears Mark 1:12 is the only place in the New Testament where the Greek word for *drove* is used in this particular manner.

It is the last part of this definition that bothers me. These words (with a force he cannot resist) do not fit the rest of the narrative we have about Jesus and the Holy Spirit. The first part of the definition is much more consistent with what is found in Matthew and Luke. It is also much more consistent with the ministry of Jesus. Of course, we do not have the liberty of splitting this definition to meet our desires.

Nothing else in the life of Jesus fits with the idea of Him being forced to do something. Jesus was not forced to die for us. He gave His life freely!

> *"Therefore, My Father loves Me, because I lay down My life that I may take it again. No one takes it from Me, but I lay it down of Myself. I have power to lay it down, and I have power to take it again. This command I have received from My Father." (John 10:17-18 – NKJV)*

When studying a subject such as this, my conclusions are often based on my training and experience as a Biblical theologian. In more familiar terms, I am constantly comparing Scripture with Scripture to resolve any conflicts. We must always compare the other things we know about the Holy Spirit with any statement we find, such as this one in the book of Mark. I conclude that the first part of the definition is the one Mark intended.

The Greek word for **led**, used in Luke 4:1, means to move or impel.[10] Yet, the translators chose the word led.

The Greek word for **led**, found in Matthew 4:1, simply means to lead.[11]

As you can see, various translators have made choices regarding these words. Invariably there can be a bias based on the particular theological position of a translator. Some would accuse me of the same type of bias. My response is that at least my position is solidly based on the rest of Scripture.

In fairness to all of the translators and Mark, I believe a common effort was made to show just how strongly Jesus felt He must go through this time of testing in the wilderness. It was perhaps something He might have preferred not to do. I have no problem making this statement. A great deal of what Jesus experienced was fraught with unpleasantness. The most notable of these is the crucifixion. It was worse than unpleasant. We have an incredible account of Jesus in the Garden of Gethsemane before He was crucified. It tells us a lot about His willingness to do things for us that were extremely difficult.

> *And He was withdrawn from them about a stone's throw, and He knelt down and prayed, saying, "Father, if it is Your will, take this cup away from Me; nevertheless, not My will, but Yours, be done." Then an angel appeared to Him from heaven, strengthening Him. And being in agony, He prayed more earnestly. Then His sweat became like great drops of blood falling down to the ground. (Luke 22:41-44 – NKJV)*

I have given you much to consider on this subject of Jesus being led or driven into the wilderness. My fundamental objective is not how this impacts the rest of this story. **My real concern is how you relate to the Holy Ghost in your life.**

Do you ever feel like the Holy Ghost is forcing you to do something? Do you make decisions or choices because you feel or sense some unseen pressure? If your answer is yes, I want to assure you this is not the way the Holy Ghost usually deals with people. Remember, He was depicted like a dove and not some aggressive or forceful animal.

I hope you have heard of the concept of being led by the Spirit as it relates to your daily life. If you have, I hope you also know how to do this. If not, then I trust you will learn a lot about it from the pages of this book. As I close out this chapter, I will provide a short synopsis of what I have written.

Does the Holy Spirit lead, or does the Holy Spirit drive or force people to do things? Will the Holy Spirit ever force you to do anything?

**The Holy Spirit is a leader. He is a guide.
He will never force you to do anything.
That is not His nature!**

Why is this relevant to the story of the temptation of Jesus?

Jesus is not only our Savior and our Lord; He is also our great example - in all things important. This makes it essential to know how this experience happened in the life of Jesus. After all, the wilderness temptation did involve the devil. We can learn much from the way Jesus spoke to the devil. We can also learn from how it all began.

If the devil could force Jesus to do something, he certainly could force us to do things. The devil had nothing to do with Jesus being in the wilderness. The Holy Ghost led Him there.

If the Holy Ghost would lead or could lead Jesus into temptation, where does this put us? Does the Holy Spirit do this to us? **Or did this event have a singular purpose?** Do you see how easily this could get twisted in the mind of a person who does not know the Word of God?

> *Let no one say when he is tempted, "I am tempted by God"; for God cannot be tempted by evil, nor does He Himself tempt anyone. But each one is tempted when he is drawn away by his own desires and enticed. Then, when desire has conceived, it gives birth to sin; and sin, when it is full-grown, brings forth death. (James 1:13-15 – NKJV)*

Many people believe God is the source of their problems. I am not necessarily talking about people who have never been saved. My reference is to people who are born-again. They have been taught the wrong doctrine. They believe God will put sickness and disease on them. They will tell you that God is the reason for calamities. They think God causes babies to die and people to be killed in accidents.

It may be hard to understand how any Christian could think this way about God. I will readily admit to you that it is hard for me to understand. It is just that I know why this type of thinking is preached. This all begins because people do not do what they are instructed to do.

> *Be diligent to present yourself approved to God, a worker who does not need to be ashamed, rightly dividing the word of truth. (2 Timothy 2:15 – NKJV)*

At this very moment, I am helping you to rightly divide the word of truth. This is a lot of work, but it is also fun. And the rewards for doing this are immense. Always remember, if you think you have found a contradiction between Scriptures, there is something you do not yet understand about one passage or the other. It could be both.

Let's go one step further before we dive deeper into the story of Jesus and the devil in the wilderness. No matter where you read this story, you will probably find the use of the word temptation. This has been the approach taken with this story for hundreds of years. Is there a better word to use? Could we resolve a lot of wrong ideas if we exchanged the word temptation for another word? Could this be justified?

A great place to start is defining the word temptation, as found in James chapter one. Then we will define the word temptation as it is found in the Gospels where our story is recorded.

We should first determine if these authors use the same Greek word. If so, then we absolutely must consider the different ways in which this word is used.

For the sake of clarity, I will repeat the verse from the book of James.

> *Let no one say when he is tempted, "I am tempted by God." (James 1:13 – KJV)*

This seems like such a simple issue. Was James using a different word for tempted? The answer is no. Much to my dismay, all four authors have used the same Greek word for tempted. So, as we proceed into this next part of the study, remember what I have said about comparing Scripture with Scripture. This is how we will decide which definition of the Greek word for tempted is appropriate.

Chapter 8
Trust and Obey

The story of the temptation of Jesus in the wilderness is one with which many people seem to be familiar. However, I am using the word "familiar" because the opinions about what happened and why vary considerably. I must confess, when I have thought about what some have claimed to be the purpose for those weeks Jesus spent in the wilderness, it has been a real shock. I have no doubt these ideas are the result of the way various individuals have taught the story over the years. But we must never adjust the Biblical narrative to suit our otherwise unsubstantiated opinions. Doing so leads to significant errors and erodes our trust in the Bible as our final rule of faith and practice. The Bible should change us and not the other way around.

Why did the Holy Spirit lead Jesus into the wilderness? What was the purpose of this event? Does the reason for this event in the life of Jesus have any meaning to you and me? These are the right questions.

In the last chapter, I began by showing what did not happen to Jesus as He entered the wilderness. This is why I made such a big deal out of the words led and driven. The shortest distance to discovering what something **is** can often be achieved by beginning a quest to figure out what it **is not**.

Jesus was not forced (against His will) to go into the wilderness. This was not designed and orchestrated by the Holy Spirit as a character-building experience for Jesus. Jesus had spent thirty years of His life growing, maturing, and developing His character. The Bible says so!

> *And Jesus increased in wisdom and in stature and in favor with God and man. (Luke 2:52 – ESV)*

There is no place in Scripture where we are told God uses the devil to cause us to be better people. I know some teach this idea. It is not true. Our interaction with the devil is very clearly defined. One of the great examples is the explanation by the apostle Paul in Ephesians chapter 6 of what is known as the armor of God. In this passage of Scripture, we are clearly instructed on how to deal with our enemy.

> *Therefore, take up the whole armor of God, that you may be able to withstand in the evil day, and having done all, to stand. (Ephesians 6:13 – NKJV)*

Absolutely nothing in the description of our armor even hints at the notion that we will grow and benefit in some character development way by using this great armor. The armor is designed to cause us to win and defeat the devil.

Our character develops
as we put the armor on, not as we use it.

When Peter and James spoke of Christians and the devil, they were also unequivocal in their instructions.

Be sober, be vigilant; because your adversary the devil walks about like a roaring lion, seeking whom he may devour. Resist him, steadfast in the faith, knowing that the same sufferings are experienced by your brotherhood in the world. (1 Peter 5:8-9 – NKJV)

Therefore, submit to God. Resist the devil and he will flee from you. (James 4:7 – NKJV)

Jesus traveled this road before us. We learn from Him and not the other way around. Since we have this ability to resist the devil and see him flee from us because we have been redeemed by the blood of Jesus, then most certainly, the sinless Jesus already had the same ability. The wilderness story proves my point.

Our preconceived assumptions make a huge difference in the way we view this milestone in the life of Jesus. I believe it was a milestone because there is no record of this ever happening again. This was a significant event in the life of Jesus. It was a time for Him to prove He knew who He was. But as you will see, it was much more than this.

It was an opportunity for Jesus to demonstrate to the devil the strength of character, resolve, and commitment that resided in Him. It was to show His determination to do the will of the Father. This experience demonstrated to the devil, and all of his demonic forces how firmly rooted these things were in the Son of God.

The wilderness temptation was a much greater problem for the devil than it was for Jesus.

The temptation of Jesus was not designed for character development. It was for a powerful display of a strong character that already existed in Jesus. Neither was it to develop a stronger resolve to do the will of the Father. It was to show the devil just how firm this resolve had already become.

I don't think anyone can read this story in any of the Gospels and not view it as a face-to-face battle between good and evil. This was a showdown between the devil and God come to earth in human flesh. The devil had been face-to-face with Jesus before, but not in human flesh. This must have been an incredible experience for the devil and one he has never forgotten.

The devil may have begun this temptation thinking he could convince Jesus to sin since He was now a man. When it was over, the devil knew just how sinless, pure, and holy the Lord Jesus is. All effort to deceive Jesus was stripped from the devil's arsenal during those days he spent in the wilderness with Jesus.

Beginning this chapter in this manner is for a specific purpose. I thought it best to start this discussion with clear statements about how I view this story and then back it up with why. I am not interested in taking portions of the story and using them to shore up some idea that has nothing to do with this event.

You may have noticed something which I think is rather revealing. The deeper we look into the life of Jesus and the things which happened to Him, the more significant the events become. By significant, I mean that as we progress, each event shows us more of the fundamental nature of the character of Jesus.

From the birth of Jesus to the crucifixion, Jesus transitioned from being surrounded by many people who adored Him to finally being alone. At His birth, Jesus shared the spotlight with His parents, the angels, the shepherds, and the wise men. In the temple experience, the spotlight is on Jesus and the doctors in the temple and, ultimately, on his parents.

When Jesus was baptized in water, the attention was shared with John the Baptist and the others who were baptized. Yes, the experience concluded in the most phenomenal way possible. The Holy Trinity was there.

In the wilderness, Jesus was left alone to face the devil by Himself. It was only at the end of the wilderness experience that the angels came to minister to Jesus. This was a precursor of things to come. At the crucifixion, when Jesus was hanging on the cross, it appears the angels had left Him. Once His side was pierced, there is no mention of the angels. He died alone for you and me. The angels are not seen again until the resurrection. This adds great meaning to these words Jesus spoke from the cross just minutes before He died.

> *And about the ninth hour Jesus cried out with a loud voice, saying, "Eli, Eli, lama sabachthani?" that is, "My God, My God, why have You forsaken Me?" (Matthew 27:46 – NKJV)*

In this context, I want to consider the rest of the story of the temptation of Jesus in the wilderness. I will provide the full text in each of the Biblical accounts of this wilderness experience.

> *Then Jesus was led up by the Spirit into the wilderness to be tempted by the devil. And when He had fasted forty days and forty nights, afterward He was hungry. Now when the tempter came to Him, he said, "If You are the Son of God, command that these stones become bread." But He answered and said, "It is written, 'Man shall not live by bread alone, but by every word that proceeds from the mouth of God.' " Then the devil took Him up into the holy city, set Him on the pinnacle of the temple, and said to Him, "If You are the Son of God, throw Yourself down. For it is written: 'He shall give His angels charge over you,' and, 'In their hands they shall bear you up, Lest you dash your foot against a stone.' " Jesus said to him, "It is written again, 'You shall not tempt the LORD your God.' " Again, the devil took Him up on an exceedingly high mountain, and showed Him all the kingdoms of the world and their glory. And he said to Him, "All these things I will give You if You will fall down and worship me." Then Jesus said to him, "Away with you, Satan! For it is written, 'You shall worship the LORD your God, and Him only you shall serve.' " Then the devil left Him, and behold, angels came and ministered to Him. (Matthew 4:1-11 – NKJV)*

There are certain things included in the account of the temptation of Jesus which were provided to us by Matthew, which I find very important. Some of these are not included by the other writers.

First, Matthew states *Jesus was led up by the Spirit into the wilderness to be tempted by the devil.* In one sentence, Matthew has told us both how Jesus came to be in the wilderness and why He was there. I have emphasized the fact that Jesus was led into the wilderness and not somehow forced to be there.

Here are some things we should consider on being led by the Spirit. This is an essential part of the Christian life. It has everything to do with our interaction with the Holy Ghost.

Learning how to be led by the Spirit is necessary for every Christian. When Jesus was teaching the disciples about the Holy Ghost, He made this statement.

> *However, when He, the Spirit of truth, has come, He will guide you into all truth; for He will not speak on His own authority, but whatever He hears He will speak; and He will tell you things to come. (John 16:13 – NKJV)*

If we are going to be guided by the Spirit into all truth, we need to know how to be led by the guide.

Jesus was a teacher. He was always teaching, both with His words and His actions. In this singular action, Jesus taught us to follow what the Spirit of God leads us to do, even when we know it may be unpleasant.

Every believer has shied away from the leading of the Spirit of God at one point or another. The anticipation of something they did not want to face prompted this decision. When I have done this, I found myself wondering why I assumed things would go badly.

I probably felt like I had sufficient evidence to draw these conclusions. Perhaps it was my lack of understanding of a previous experience.

Wonder what would happen if we faced every leading of the Holy Ghost with absolute confidence that the results would turn into something good? This is precisely what Jesus did. He knew the Holy Spirit was not leading Him into a place where He would suffer defeat.

The greatest need for those involved in the Great Awakening is knowing how to be led by the Spirit of God. When I say knowing how, I include the boldness and confidence to be led by the Spirit without fear of the consequences. I am speaking of a level of trust in the Holy Ghost that many people do not have.

Trust is always a part of being led.

The trust goes both ways. I must trust myself in my ability to hear the voice of God. I must trust myself to know the Holy Ghost with such great confidence that I do not hesitate to follow Him. This is a very personal relationship. It is a relationship built on trust.

While I must trust myself, it is also true that I must trust the Holy Ghost. I must believe the Holy Ghost knows me. As long as I am inclined to believe the Holy Ghost might do things to hurt me or put me in a place where I could get hurt because He did not tell me everything I needed to know, I will not trust Him. Neither will you. As long as I think the Holy Ghost might purposely embarrass and humiliate me, I will not trust Him. Neither will you.

Jesus knew the Holy Spirit could be trusted. Whatever it might mean to be tempted by the devil was obviously of no real concern to Jesus. We see no signs of resistance in the life of Jesus in any of the accounts we have been given in the Gospels as He approached this experience. Jesus was teaching us about the Holy Ghost.

We can develop this same level of confidence in being led by the Spirit. It is something that happens slowly over a period of time. It begins with easy instructions.

One day I was driving down one of the major streets in Tulsa, Oklahoma. I was thirsty and stopped at a convenience store to purchase something to drink. As I came out of the store, I heard the voice of the Spirit of God telling me to get in my pick-up truck and leave that area of town immediately. He told me I was in danger.

As I hurried to my truck, I glanced around. I saw nothing alarming. I obeyed anyway. When I started the engine, I left the area as quickly and safely as possible.

This does raise some questions. How did I know this was the voice of the Spirit? I was confident it was the Holy Spirit because He has spoken to me many times since childhood. Everything has gone well every time I have listened and followed His leadership. The opposite result was my experience when I did not follow what the Holy Ghost said to me. This is the part that takes time.

Everybody wants to know if the store got robbed or if something else terrible happened. If you happen to be thinking in this manner, ask yourself why these matter to you.

Why is it important. to have those answers? Is it because this is how you have become accustomed to determining if you have heard the voice of the Spirit? Don't feel bad if it is. You are not alone. Just consider what this approach means. Taking such an approach indicates we have judged our ability to hear the voice of the Holy Ghost by whether or not something we expected to happen did indeed happen. An approach of this nature is not reliable.

We are talking about trust.

Being led by the Spirit does not leave room for our assumptions. Nothing bad happened when this experience occurred. Perhaps it was my obedience that kept anything terrible from happening. Once again, this is a matter of trust. It really does not matter if I ever know why I was told to leave this place immediately.

Many times, I have explicitly been led by the Spirit to pray for a sick person. I did what I was instructed to do, and nothing happened. To some, this means I missed God. According to some observers, I was not hearing the voice of the Holy Ghost. Such a conclusion implies or assumes I was the only one who had something to do with the sick person receiving their healing.

It is rare (very rare) that we are ever alone in following the voice of the Holy Ghost and being led by Him. There is almost always at least one or more parties involved. We must learn to do our part, even if the other party does not. I heard a man who often prays for the sick in public places say he prayed for about 1000 people before any of them got healed.

This man went on to say that he was doing what God told him to do, so he kept doing it and he has had great results.

That is an excellent example of being led by the Spirit. That brother has developed a great trust in his ability to hear from God, and he is still growing.

Jesus had absolute confidence in His ability to hear His Father's voice. We should too.

Next, I will call your attention to the meaning of the word temptation as we find it in this story. This is the definition given for the Greek word for **temptation**.

To try or test one's faith, virtue, or character, by enticement to sin; hence, according to the content equivalent to solicit to sin, to tempt; James 1:13; Galatians 6:1; Revelation 2:10; of the temptations of the devil, Matthew 4:1,3; Luke 4:2; 1Corinthians 7:5; 1 Thessalonians 3:5[12]

The first Scripture mentioned is James 1:13. From what this verse and the one that follows it says, it is clear that James was speaking of the temptation to sin.

> *Let no one say when he is tempted, "I am tempted of God"; for God cannot be tempted by evil, nor does He Himself tempt anyone. But each one is tempted when he is drawn away by his own desires and enticed. (James 1:14 – NKJV)*

Jesus was not drawn into this situation in the wilderness with the devil by His own desires. Jesus had no desire to sin. Jesus was led into the wilderness by the Holy Ghost. If there was any enticement to sin during this entire experience, it did not originate with Jesus. The enticement and effort to create the wrong desires would have emanated from the devil.

There are basic questions that must be answered to understand what this time in the wilderness was really all about. Perhaps you have thought of this and may have arrived at your own answers. I must tell you I have never heard one sermon about the time Jesus spent in the wilderness that answered the following questions.

In each of the three temptations presented by the devil, which part of it was a sin if Jesus did it? Some have assumed the only sin would have been for Jesus to do anything the devil said. They speak of this story as though this is all it amounted to. But was there a deeper, more profound issue involved? For example, was it a sin for Jesus to make bread out of rocks? Or, was the sin something that had nothing to do with making bread? If that is the case, then why did the devil draw attention to the bread? Since Jesus was hungry couldn't that be seen as a kind gesture?

These are the questions I will answer in the next chapter. The answers are simple, but they may still surprise you.

Chapter 9
No Bread for Me

On the surface, it appears Joseph was given conflicting information about the name of the son of God. Before Jesus was born, an angel appeared to Joseph and told him the name of this new baby boy. A casual reading of the instructions is a little confusing.

> *Now the birth of Jesus Christ was as follows: After His mother Mary was betrothed to Joseph, before they came together, she was found with child of the Holy Spirit. Then Joseph her husband, being a just man, and not wanting to make her a public example, was minded to put her away secretly. But while he thought about these things, behold, an angel of the Lord appeared to him in a dream, saying, "Joseph, son of David, do not be afraid to take to you Mary your wife, for that which is conceived in her is of the Holy Spirit. And she will bring forth a Son, and you shall call His name JESUS, for He will save His people from their sins." So all this was done that it might be fulfilled which was spoken by the Lord through the prophet, saying: "Behold, the virgin shall be with child, and bear a Son, and they shall call His name*

Immanuel," *which is translated, "God with us."* *(Matthew 1:18-23 – NKJV)*

How was Joseph to reconcile the difference between these two names? Why didn't the angel say to name the baby Immanuel? This is what had been prophesied. The angel made it very clear that this prophecy's fulfillment was important.

What matters is the meaning of these two names. This is best understood by combining them.

His name is Immanuel Jesus.

I don't think I have ever heard Jesus called by this name. We call Him Jesus. We call Him Emmanuel. We sing about both of these names, and I love every moment of it. I am not saying there is anything wrong with this. But by definition, His name is *God with us for He will save His people from their sins.*

When Jesus was born, God came to earth in the form of a human baby. When Jesus breathed His first breath of earth's air, God was here in visible, touchable form. He came on an assignment from His Father with a very specific purpose.

The Son of God was born on this earth to save His people from their sins. This was God in human flesh who had come to bring salvation to us. At no time in His life did Jesus ever veer off course. Every time Jesus heard His name, He was hearing that He was God. Every time Jesus heard His name, He heard His purpose in being on this planet.

This is the person who was led into the wilderness to be tempted of the devil. We must give this full consideration to understand what was happening in this epic event.

Let's start where Matthew begins and examine the temptation to make bread.

> *And when He had fasted forty days and forty nights, afterward He was hungry. Now when the tempter came to Him, he said, "If You are the Son of God, command that these stones become bread." But He answered and said, "It is written, 'Man shall not live by bread alone, but by every word that proceeds from the mouth of God.'* " (Matthew 4:2-4 – NKJV)*

Hunger is not a sin. Jesus had not eaten in 40 days. He had been fasting and had just ended His fast when the devil arrived. What is the temptation?

The story is cast in such a manner that it implies the temptation was making bread out of stones. With all the miracles Jesus performed later, such as turning water into wine, I am not sure this part was the actual test. Jesus could have made bread out of these rocks. Other than the suggestion coming from the devil, how would this have been different from Him making wine?

I would never even imply it is a good idea for anyone to follow a suggestion from the devil. But for this to result in sin, the suggestion must be to do something sinful. **If making wine out of water was not sinful, I fail to see anything sinful in making bread out of rocks.**

Where is the sin?

I would like for you to consider something else. The very first words of the definition I provided for tempted are the words *to try or test one's faith*. Have you ever considered the real test in this entire experience was a challenge regarding who Jesus is? Historically the focus has been on the devil trying to get Jesus to sin. But performing miracles by taking something from nature and turning it into something else is considered by many to be the first miracle in the ministry of Jesus.

Pause in your reading for a moment and think about the following statements from the devil.

Temptation #1. If You are the Son of God;

Temptation #2. If You are the Son of God;

Temptation #3. All these things I will give You if You will fall down and worship me.

Those three phrases reveal the real test going on in this story. It is much too easy to get sidetracked by the rest of the information. I am convinced this experience was all about one thing. But it has two parts. I will share them both by asking the same question in several ways.

Did Jesus know who He was? Did Jesus know He was the Son of God? Was Jesus convinced, beyond any doubt, He was the Son of God? Did Jesus feel any need to prove He was the Son of God? Did Jesus believe what the voice from Heaven had said when Jesus was baptized?

> *And behold, a voice from heaven said, "This is my beloved Son, with whom I am well pleased." (Matthew 3:17 – ESV)*

Everything in the life of Jesus, from His birth all the way through His water baptism experience, had been building up to this moment. And Jesus was fully prepared. It had been 40 days since that exhilarating moment when Jesus heard the voice of His Father. Was Jesus still willing to stake everything on the fact that He believed these stories about how He was conceived? An actual voice, the voice of His Father, had spoken to Him from heaven. Did Jesus believe that voice?

This goes to the very heart of the first two temptations as the story is presented in the gospel of Matthew. Of course, there is a third test.

Forget about what the devil promised if Jesus would worship him. The devil did not own any of the things he promised Jesus, and he had no power or ability to give them to Jesus.

This has confused a lot of knowledgeable people. They have openly declared that the devil had to be able to give these things to Jesus, or it was not a real temptation. If we do not take into consideration certain Scriptures, this makes sense. Yet it raises some fundamental questions. Did Jesus not know or remember He was present at the creation of all things? As much of the Old Testament as Jesus knew, had He forgotten these words?

> *The earth is the Lord's, and the fulness thereof; the world, and they that dwell therein. For he hath founded it upon the seas, and established it upon the floods. Who shall ascend into the hill of the Lord? or who shall stand in his holy place? (Psalm 24:1-3 – KJV)*

Nothing in the Bible even implies the ownership of this Earth, and everything on it has ever been the devil's property.

It has never belonged to man. Everything belongs to God. It always has, and it always will. Otherwise, God has no right to destroy the Earth.

> *But the day of the Lord will come as a thief in the night, in which the heavens will pass away with a great noise, and the elements will melt with fervent heat; both the earth and the works that are in it will be burned up. Therefore, since all these things will be dissolved, what manner of persons ought you to be in holy conduct and godliness, looking for and hastening the coming of the day of God, because of which the heavens will be dissolved, being on fire, and the elements will melt with fervent heat?*
> *(2 Peter 3:10-12 – NKJV)*

Others may be willing to say Jesus did not know these things. I certainly am not. There is tremendous evidence of the vast knowledge Jesus had. I see no Biblical reason to believe the devil had the right and the authority to do what he promised he would do in return for Jesus falling down and worshiping him. This brings up another fascinating question.

At this point in the life of Jesus, had the Holy Ghost not revealed to Him that the devil is a liar? If not, then this completely changes the status of things with regard to the Holy Ghost, putting Jesus in this predicament. At no other time in the life of Jesus do we have the slightest hint that He was unprepared.

So, I believe Jesus knew the devil was a liar.

Jesus was fully aware of who He was dealing with in the wilderness. He knew all about the devil. Jesus knew the devil was lying. Remember, it was Jesus who later uttered these words.

> *You are of your father the devil, and the desires of your father you want to do. He was a murderer from the beginning, and does not stand in the truth, because there is no truth in him. When he speaks a lie, he speaks from his own resources, for he is a liar and the father of it. (John 8:44 – NKJV)*

If Jesus did not know this before He went into the wilderness, when did He discover this essential truth? For the Father to allow Jesus to be subjected to this testing without the proper preparation depicts a God I do not know. Had Jesus been a rebellious Son, unwilling to listen and learn, that might be different. We must remember that the Father had said He was well pleased with Jesus. Admittedly we have no record of when or how Jesus learned many of the things He knew. We can only assume this was a great part of Jesus growing in wisdom, and knowledge and stature with God.

What was the real test?

Did Jesus know that He (Jesus) was the one who should be worshiped? It would be one thing for Jesus to be convinced He was the Son of God. But, did Jesus believe He was God? Did Jesus think He should be worshiped? Unequivocally Jesus knew He was the Son of God.

Let's address the question of worshiping Jesus while He was on this earth in human form. I am specifically talking about the period of time before the crucifixion and resurrection. Did people worship Jesus? Did Jesus allow it?

The angels did not allow people to worship them. The prophets of the Old Testament were not worshiped. So, this is a valid question, especially in light of the statement Jesus made to the devil about who we should worship.

There are many examples of people kneeling before Jesus during the years of His earthly ministry. Often these were acts of thanksgiving for a healing or a miracle Jesus had performed. It is commonly accepted that kneeling is an act of worship.

However, there is one Scripture that stands out to me. We find some extraordinary wording after Jesus had calmed the wind and the waves and Peter had walked on the water towards Jesus. As you will recall, Peter was drowning, and Jesus saved his life. Then we have a very specific record of the worship of Jesus.

> *Then those who were in the boat came and worshiped Him, saying, "Truly You are the Son of God."* (Matthew 14:33 – NKJV)

By His answer, Jesus made it clear that He knew He was the one to receive worship. He not only knew it; He boldly declared it to the devil.

> *Then saith Jesus unto him, Get thee hence, Satan: for it is written, Thou shalt worship the Lord thy God, and him only shalt thou serve. (Matthew 4:10 – KJV)*

Now the devil had a much bigger problem. Something else was revealed in the wilderness. Not only did Jesus know who He was and that He was deserving of worship, something else had become too obvious to ignore.

The devil now knew beyond a shadow of a doubt that this was the Son of God.

The greatest fear the devil had known up to that moment had just hit him in full force. What the disciples were to learn much later, the devil already knew.

> *And He said to them, "I saw Satan fall like lightning from heaven. Behold, I give you the authority to trample on serpents and scorpions, and over all the power of the enemy, and nothing shall by any means hurt you. (Luke 10:18-19 – NKJV)*

The devil had just confirmed what he secretly suspected. This was the one, standing right in front of him in a human body, who was there the day he got thrown out of Heaven! The devil never expected to find Jesus on this earth as a man, certainly not a man who knew about his past before he was thrown out of heaven. No wonder the devil left Him.

Can you imagine what a blow this must have been to the devil? Don't be concerned. I don't feel sorry for the devil, not even for a moment. He had tried in different ways to kill this man they called Jesus. None of that had worked. It was now time to start another plan.

I will discuss this plan in the following chapters. However, I must first share a few things regarding the other records of the wilderness temptation.

The account given by Mark of the temptation of Jesus in the wilderness will come next. It provides things we did not see in the account given by Matthew. Then I will follow with an in-depth look at what Luke has recorded. So, prepare yourself for more revelation knowledge.

Chapter 10
Jump

Why did the devil take three completely different approaches when he tested Jesus? It is obvious that he did. But why? Does this three-pronged approach have any significance to us? The following comments may provoke a strong reaction from some of the more astute students of the Bible who still do not understand the nature of man.

Earlier in this book, I mentioned that man is a spirit; he has a soul and lives in a body. This is a common view of certain groups of Christians. It is evident that, to some degree, the devil knew this about Jesus. Since the devil is a creature of the world of the spirit, perhaps this was obvious to him. The devil could see His body and perhaps His spirit. I believe the devil views us in much the same way.

It all goes back to those three temptations. Why were there three and only three? They were starkly different tests. Each seems to have been designed to test Jesus in a particular fashion. If this is correct, what was it?

The writer of the Book of Hebrews made the following observation about Jesus.

Seeing then that we have a great High Priest who has passed through the heavens, Jesus the Son of God, let us hold fast our confession. For we do not have a High Priest who cannot sympathize with our weaknesses, but was in all points tempted as we are, yet without sin. (Hebrews 4:14-15 – NKJV)

The last phrase in these verses is very interesting. Jesus was in all points tempted as we are, yet without sin. Precisely what does that mean? Does it relate to the temptation of Jesus in the wilderness? Does it have anything to do with my questions about these temptations?

Let's combine this information to arrive at our conclusion.

Man is a three-part being.

- These three parts are spirit, soul, and body.

- Jesus was tempted in all points as we are yet without sin.

- There were three different temptations.

Each temptation must have been directed at a different point, or that is to say, there was one temptation of the body, one of the soul, and one of the spirit.

If I am correct and can show which temptation is directed at each of these areas, we have the answers to many questions about this dramatic experience.

I have included all three accounts of the temptation story in the chapters of this book. **Surely we can agree that the temptation to turn rocks into bread was a temptation**

directed at the body of Jesus. Jesus was hungry. Maybe He could be tempted to sin with His body. Now, this does create an interesting challenge.

If turning rocks into bread is not a sin, and I have said that it can't be, how could this be a sin of the body of Jesus?

The devil had thousands of years of experience tempting the bodies of other humans to sin. Many things listed in the Bible as sin involve the body and the mind. All perversion and immorality involve both. But the devil knew he was dealing with a different kind of human body. This one came from only one human parent. The other part was the work of the Holy Spirit. Before he attempted to get to the spirit of Jesus and cause sin at that level, the devil wanted to test the vulnerability of this amazing human body.

I think most Christians know that Jesus was both God and man. This is called the hypostatic union, and it is inexplicable. This is one of those things we accept by faith. There is evidence of it in the ministry of Jesus. There is extensive discussion of it in the Bible. I will emphatically declare this union to be true. At the same time, I will not attempt to prove it or explain it. Plenty of others have tried and failed.

My discussion about this aspect of the life of Jesus has a purpose. I believe the devil wanted to know what he would be dealing with in his encounters with Jesus. Was this God? Was this the Son of God? Was this a man? He looked to be every bit a man. So, what part of Him was the most vulnerable?

The devil had often presented a seemingly harmless temptation to the bodies of men and women. Desiring things they should not have, especially when no other person would know, was a common temptation used by the devil. Because they had fallen for this trap, this had destroyed the lives of millions of people.

Was this human susceptible?

I can imagine the devil saying to himself, "He is hungry. I will challenge Him to make bread. Then I will find out how much control the God part of this person has over the human part. This will show me if He is indeed the Son of God." "Is He the son of God? If so, does He know this for certain? Is His human side able to overpower His God side?" That last question applies to all three temptations. No person on earth knew these answers except Jesus. I wonder if the devil was aware of this fact.

I spoke about the temptation to turn rocks into bread. And I talked about the temptation regarding the devil's offer to give Jesus authority over the things he showed to Him. I have written a few things about those two temptations prior to my discussion of the three types of temptation. And I plan to say more.

But for now, I will now skip over the part of Jesus, which was His soul, and cover that last. It should be obvious which temptation was directed at the spirit of Jesus. It was the temptation to worship the devil. I am basing my conclusion on these statements made by Jesus.

On one occasion, Jesus encountered a woman from Samaria, where Jesus had stopped at a well to get a drink of water. They struck up a conversation. When Jesus pointed out the sin in the woman's life, she attempted to change the subject. This is where we will pick up the story.

> *The woman saith unto him, Sir, I perceive that thou art a prophet. Our fathers worshiped in this mountain; and ye say, that in Jerusalem is the place where men ought to worship. Jesus saith unto her, Woman, believe me, the hour cometh, when ye shall neither in this mountain, nor yet at Jerusalem, worship the Father. Ye worship ye know not what: we know what we worship: for salvation is of the Jews. But the hour cometh, and now is, when the true worshipers shall worship the Father in spirit and in truth: for the Father seeketh such to worship him. God is a Spirit: and they that worship him must worship him in spirit and in truth. (John 4:19-24 – KJV)*

The connection between worship and the spirit is evident in the words of Jesus. The devil had observed how firmly and deeply these two things were connected. He must have assumed that if he could get Jesus to worship him, he could break the connection between God and the Son of God. I seriously doubt he expected Jesus to know that He, the Son of God, was the one to receive the worship. After all, He appeared only to be a man. This was the devil's first opportunity to experience the power of the human spirit when it was in right standing with God. **The devil had no idea this opportunity to be in right standing with God would be made available to every man, woman, boy, and girl on this planet who receives Jesus as Lord and Savior.**

This leaves one other temptation for us to consider. We must also discover the connection it had to the soul of Jesus.

I have not written anything about this third temptation. So first, I will share my thoughts about the temptation.

> *Then the devil took Him up into the holy city, set Him on the pinnacle of the temple, and said to Him, "If You are the Son of God, throw Yourself down. For it is written: 'He shall give His angels charge over you,' and, 'In their hands they shall bear you up, Lest you dash your foot against a stone.' " Jesus said to him, "It is written again, 'You shall not tempt the LORD your God.' "*
> *(Matthew 4:5-7 – NKJV)*

> *Then he brought Him to Jerusalem, set Him on the pinnacle of the temple, and said to Him, "If You are the Son of God, throw Yourself down from here. For it is written: 'He shall give His angels charge over you, To keep you,' and, 'In their hands they shall bear you up, Lest you dash your foot against a stone.' " And Jesus answered and said to him, "It has been said, 'You shall not tempt the LORD your God.' "*
> *(Luke 4:9-12 – NKJV)*

My initial reaction is the same every time I read this. I hope I don't offend you, but I wonder. Did the devil really believe Jesus was nuts? Why would any sane person do what the devil suggested to Jesus? And my subsequent reaction is pretty good. Why does anyone ever do what the devil has suggested? Every idea the devil has is crazy. Yet millions of people follow his suggestions every day. Some of these are highly intelligent and highly educated people.

This was a temptation of the soul of Jesus.

The soul of man encompasses the mind, the thoughts, the imagination, the feelings, and the emotions of a person. Was Jesus any different from the other people the devil had tempted? He had suggested many things to people, and they did them, even though they were ridiculous. Millions of lives had been destroyed because they followed through on some crazy idea the devil suggested.

You are probably aware that there is a branch of our military known as paratroopers. I have a dear friend who was at one time a paratrooper. They train extensively for what they do. They jump out of airplanes hundreds of times, practicing pinpoint landings. But they don't just jump out of airplanes, the safety training involved is meticulous. In wartime, this has proven to be an effective way to get behind enemy lines to rescue those who were trapped or cause significant damage to the enemy.

Jumping out of airplanes is not only something our military does; civilians do it for fun. I have spent millions of hours flying all over the United States in many different airplanes. Not once have I been tempted to jump out. If this is something you enjoy, God Bless you. Do it safely, and be sure you wear a parachute prepared by an expert.

This is the first problem with the last temptation. There was no parachute. Jesus was challenged to prove He was the Son of God by jumping from the pinnacle of the temple with nothing to protect Him in case the angels decided not to get involved. In my opinion, He proved He was the Son of God by not jumping. I know I have not talked about the angels. I will explain their role in the next chapter.

First, I want to be sure you understand why I said this was a test of the soul. Was the mind of Jesus inclined to do stupid things or dangerous things? If Jesus was the Son of God, then He would not be given to ridiculous thoughts, especially regarding things that would put Him in danger. Some people scale the outside of skyscrapers with no protection. I am not trying to be offensive, but there is something amiss in that mind. What would be the sin involved in Jesus jumping from the pinnacle of the temple and expecting the angels to catch Him?

I have several thoughts to share with you. I have said the test was about whether Jesus knew who He was. I am not changing my mind. The devil was willing to do anything necessary to figure out who this man was. However, this test generates different questions. What did Jesus know about the angels? Did Jesus understand the role of the angels better than the devil did? Remember, the devil was once an angel. He is one of the three angels mentioned by name in the Bible.

The devil knew the activity he suggested for the angels was outside the purview of their assignment. Yes, even where Jesus was concerned. Angels will protect us and keep watch over us. They will intervene when we do things we should not do. However, this suggestion was beyond reasonable. The devil attempted to quote Scripture to make this enticing. He even failed in his quotation. The statement from the devil reads as follows in Matthew's account.

He shall give His angels charge over you,' and, 'In their hands they shall bear you up, Lest you dash your foot against a stone.' (Matthew 4:6 – NKJV)

Luke has added a short phrase to his account.

*'He shall give His angels charge over you, To keep you,'
and, 'In their hands they shall bear you up, Lest you dash
your foot against a stone.' (Luke 4:10-11 – NKJV)*

The actual verse from Psalm 91 reads as follows.

*For He shall give His angels charge over you, To keep
you in all your ways. In their hands they shall bear
you up, Lest you dash your foot against a stone.
(Psalms 91:11-12 – NKJV)*

The quote from Luke is the closer of the two when compared to Psalm 91. However, in both instances, the words, *in all your ways,* were left out. If the devil had included those words, Jesus could have immediately responded by telling the devil that jumping off the temple's pinnacle was not one of those ways. Common sense prevented it.

Every day people do foolish things, knowing it is ridiculous. I mean, no offense, but God has given us common sense, and He expects us to use it. So do the angels.

A part of maturity is knowing how to avoid needless danger.

I have called this a temptation of the soul of Jesus because the devil was playing mind games with the Son of God. Remember the lead-in to this temptation. *If you are the Son of God,* then jump. The angels will catch you.

Did Jesus know as much about the angels as the devil did? This was one way for the devil to find out if Jesus was the Son of God. Any other person may have fallen for this, thinking the angels were compelled to protect them.

Years ago, I oversaw a large meeting in a facility that seats 20,000 people. The ceiling in this building is 60 feet high. In the middle of one of the services, I spotted a man who had climbed up on a steel beam over the audience.

This steel support beam was about 50 feet in the air. And here was this man clinging to the beam for dear life. You can imagine what was going through my mind.

I sent a crew to help him get down from his perch. Someone called the local police, and they arrested the man for endangering the public. I asked permission to speak to the man before they took him away. He seemed to talk like an average person. He wasn't mentally ill, but something was wrong. He said God challenged him to climb out on this beam. I told him it was not God. I am still not sure how a person could arrive at such a conclusion. He had endangered a lot of people. The man was greatly deceived.

Jesus could not be deceived. He was, and He is, the Son of God. He is completely God, and He is completely man. A man in whom there has never been any sin.

The wisdom which had been growing in Jesus prevailed that day. It was not a difficult decision for Jesus to decline the foolishness of the devil. From this, we can learn a great deal about life.

Once again, we benefit from our example. On the surface, these challenges faced by Jesus in the wilderness may seem small or unimportant. But how many people do you know who have wrecked their lives by yielding to one foolish suggestion? If it is only one person, that is too many. Jesus never gave in and neither should we.

Chapter 11
Angels in the Wilderness

Mark had a habit of using the word immediately. In the following Scripture passage, I include Mark's account of the water baptism of Jesus to show his use of this word. The text reads, *And immediately, coming up from the water.* The repeated use of this word caused me to wonder what Mark was attempting to convey. The following is the complete text.

> *It came to pass in those days that Jesus came from Nazareth of Galilee, and was baptized by John in the Jordan. And immediately, coming up from the water, He saw the heavens parting and the Spirit descending upon Him like a dove. Then a voice came from heaven, "You are My beloved Son, in whom I am well pleased." Immediately the Spirit drove Him into the wilderness. And He was there in the wilderness forty days, tempted by Satan, and was with the wild beasts; and the angels ministered to Him. (Mark 1:9-13 – NKJV)*

Very little helpful information can be found in the *Greek Lexicons* regarding the word **immediately**. They mention the repeated use of the adverb, with no comments indicating why this might be the case. *Thayer* does note that the word is used 41 times in Mark's gospel.[13] In some cases, you will find the word immediately; in others, the translation will be straightway or forthwith. It is, of course, impossible to get into Mark's mind and determine his reasoning. Thus, we must assume Mark wanted to convey that there was no delay in the many miraculous events in the ministry of Jesus. This may be why many people think all miracles are instantaneous.

How is this helpful to us? If we embrace this as a norm and expect a swift response when we ask God to do something, we may, at times, be disappointed. This will not be due to a failure on God's part. God cannot fail. Not immediately getting what we want usually happens because we have overlooked other serious aspects of receiving from God. There is much more involved than just asking. James provides some helpful information.

> *You ask and do not receive, because you ask amiss,*
> *that you may spend it on your pleasures.*
> *(James 4:3 – NKJV)*

I would suggest more prayers are offered in a manner we could label as asking amiss than in any other form. James has pointed to one way of thinking about what this means. The old *King James Bible* is much more direct than some of the newer translations. This is one reason I tend to favor that translation. Compare these words with those in the *New King James Version.*

> *Ye ask, and receive not, because ye ask amiss, that ye*
> *may consume it upon your lusts. (James 4:3 – KJV)*

The Greek word translated **pleasures** or **lusts**[14] is, at the very least, indicative of something inconsistent with a truly spiritual character. It is not a stretch to say this does not have to be immoral or perverse. When Paul wrote his letter to Titus, he used this same Greek word. Paul places the word **lust** in the context of several other unacceptable things to God.

> *For we ourselves also were sometimes foolish, disobedient, deceived, serving divers lusts and pleasures, living in malice and envy, hateful, and hating one another. (Titus 3:3 – KJV)*

If any of the things listed in this verse express the condition of a person's heart when they pray, this would be asking amiss. Not only will God not answer such a prayer immediately, but He also will not answer it at all.

Long ago, the Psalmist declared the following.

> *If I regard iniquity in my heart, the Lord will not hear. (Psalm 66:18 – NKJV)*

Knowing this about God and prayer could save a lot of anxiety for thousands of people who call themselves Christians. If they would find out what is included in iniquity and rid it from their lives, they would receive many more answers to their prayers. God does want to answer us when we pray, but there are conditions to be met.

I do not mean to imply that Mark thought everything God does would happen instantaneously. What we have in Mark's writings is an example of a tremendous thrill and excitement to see what God was doing through Jesus. Many things did happen immediately.

At the beginning of this chapter, I made mention of the last six words of this story about Jesus being tempted in the wilderness. It is surprising to find additional details, especially with such a brief coverage of the event.

Here are the words: *and the angels ministered to Him.*

What exactly did the angels do?

Two significant thoughts come to mind. The first is the presence of angels throughout the life of Jesus on this earth. The angels announced the birth of Jesus and the resurrection of Jesus, and as Jesus was ascending back into Heaven, the angels announced His soon return. I am certain angels are much more involved in our lives than we realize. Let me leave you with this thought; the angels want to be even more engaged with us, and they want us to know they are always there to help us. I do not want to stray too far from my subject. So, I will continue explaining the meaning of the phrase from our story.

The second thing to consider that will help us understand what part the angels played in the temptation story is to examine another story about Jesus.

A few hours before the crucifixion, Jesus was in the garden praying. His disciples were with Him, but they were asleep. In this challenging moment, the angels came to Jesus once again.

> *Then an angel appeared to Him from heaven, strengthening Him. (Luke 22:43 – NKJV)*

No precise details are given regarding what this angel did. We must rely entirely on the meaning of another Greek word.

The word for **strengthening** means to inspirit.[15] Now we must understand what it means to inspirit.

One definition of **inspirit** is: to instill courage and life.[16] Yet another dictionary states the word means to infuse spirit or life into; enliven.[17]

These definitions provide enough information to let us know this was more than physical strengthening. It was deeply spiritual. In both cases, this would have been very appropriate. What took place was the most significant and meaningful action ever taken by a human. The experience of Jesus in the Garden of Gethsemane before the crucifixion may have been far greater than the one in the wilderness, but I am not sure how we would measure this. Both resulted in profound defeats for the devil.

What I have just shared regarding these angels is enlightening and exciting. We often only think of angels as delivering messages, singing, or being with us to provide protection. Definitely, they do all three of these things and much more. But consider this.

Throughout the pages of this book, I have drawn in the concept of Jesus as our example. Much of what Jesus did was to teach us by His example. Other things Jesus did were for the purpose of being our substitute. All of these things are important.

My effort has been to illustrate how Jesus interacted with the Holy Spirit. As we understand these things, we learn how we should interact with the Holy Spirit. We should apply this same approach to the angels.

I see no Scriptural reason to think the angels are not willing and ready to do many of the same things for us that they did for Jesus. Perhaps in your life, you could use more courage. The angels stand ready to help you have more courage.

Maybe life has been hard for you as you have gone through difficult times. The battles we face can sometimes seem to drain the life right out of us. Allow the angels to do for you what they did for Jesus in these difficult times in His life.

I dare to say, even now, angels are with you to enliven your spirit and strengthen you. Yes, they will do it!

Chapter 12
The Devil's Deal

I am devoting an entire chapter to the story of the temptation of Jesus in the wilderness as it is given to us in the gospel of Luke. Having covered the accounts in the gospel of Matthew and the gospel of Mark, I did not initially think this would be necessary. Then the Holy Spirit drew my attention to a specific difference in Luke's account, which provides the insight we did not receive from the other authors. Read the following verses carefully and see if you spot it.

> *Then Jesus, being filled with the Holy Spirit, returned from the Jordan and was led by the Spirit into the wilderness, being tempted for forty days by the devil. And in those days, He ate nothing, and afterward when they had ended, He was hungry. And the devil said to Him, "If You are the Son of God, command this stone to become bread." But Jesus answered him, saying, "It is written, 'Man shall not live by bread alone, but by every word of God.'" Then the devil, taking Him up on a high mountain, showed Him all the kingdoms of the world in a moment of time. And the devil said to Him, "All this authority I will give You, and their glory; for this has been*

delivered to me, and I give it to whomever I wish. Therefore, if You will worship before me, all will be Yours." And Jesus answered and said to him, "Get behind Me, Satan! For it is written, 'You shall worship the LORD your God, and Him only you shall serve.' " Then he brought Him to Jerusalem, set Him on the pinnacle of the temple, and said to Him, "If You are the Son of God, throw Yourself down from here. For it is written: 'He shall give His angels charge over you, To keep you,' and, 'In their hands, they shall bear you up, lest you dash your foot against a stone.' " And Jesus answered and said to him, "It has been said, 'You shall not tempt the LORD your God.' " Now when the devil had ended every temptation, he departed from Him until an opportune time. (Luke 4:1-13 – NKJV)

There are two differences between this account and the one given to us by Matthew. The first and most noticeable difference is the sequence of the three temptations. The first temptation is the same. The last two are in reverse order to what we found in the gospel of Matthew.

The second significant difference is in the offer the devil made to Jesus regarding the kingdoms of the world. The specific difference is found in this statement. Read it very carefully.

Again, the devil took Him up on an exceedingly high mountain, and showed Him all the kingdoms of the world and their glory. And he said to Him, "All these things I will give You if You will fall down and worship me." (Matthew 4:8-9 – NKJV)

136

Then the devil, taking Him up on a high mountain, showed Him all the kingdoms of the world in a moment of time. And the devil said to Him, "All this authority I will give You, and their glory; for this has been delivered to me, and I give it to whomever I wish. (Luke 4:5-6 – NKJV)

In the first reference, the devil offered to give Jesus *all these things*. This refers to the kingdoms the devil had shown to Jesus. However, it is important to note that the Greek word for **kingdoms** means the territory subject to the rule of a king.[18] I will explain this later.

In the second reference, the devil offered to give Jesus *all this authority*. This Greek word is translated as power in the *King James Version* and authority in the *New King James Version,* and it means **jurisdiction**.[19]

There are other differences I will discuss later, but I believe this is the best place to begin. When I wrote about the devil's offering to give Jesus *all these things,* I followed the common wisdom and commented as if the devil was talking about his supposed ownership of the earth. I presented a solid Biblical case for the fact that the devil does not own this earth and never has. The words used by the devil in both accounts are the words *kingdoms of the world and their glory.* A little later, I will address what this means.

In Matthew's record of this event, the devil mentioned *these things*, which is a reference to the kingdoms. The devil implied his ownership of these kingdoms and, therefore, the supposed right to give them away. I have said several times that the devil did not own this earth.

Did the devil own these kingdoms, as he has implied? In a moment, we will see.

In the gospel of Luke, the devil offered to give Jesus *all this authority*. The devil was very bold in his statements about this authority. He declared *for this has been delivered to me, and I give it to whomever I wish*. The devil claimed to have authority over these kingdoms. He wanted Jesus to believe this authority was so complete and of such a nature that he could give it to anyone. The devil had chosen Jesus as the person he wanted to give this authority to. Of course, in exchange, the devil wanted Jesus to worship him.

It is interesting that the devil never said how he got this authority. Assume for the moment he had it. All the devil was willing to reveal was that this authority had been delivered to him. Let's take this matter of authority one step at a time so there is no confusion.

On another occasion, Jesus made two fantastic statements about authority and power which we must bring into this discussion. The first passage is a record of what was said by Jesus after His resurrection. Soldiers had been paid to lie about the resurrection of Jesus and say His body was stolen from the tomb. Some people believed this lie. This is the rest of the story.

> *Then the eleven disciples went away into Galilee, to the mountain which Jesus had appointed for them. When they saw Him, they worshiped Him; but some doubted. And Jesus came and spoke to them, saying, "All authority has been given to Me in heaven and on earth. Go therefore and make disciples of all the nations, baptizing them in*

the name of the Father and of the Son and of the Holy Spirit, teaching them to observe all things that I have commanded you; and lo, I am with you always, even to the end of the age." (Matthew 28:16-20 – NKJV)

Jesus had this authority before the resurrection. Jesus said He had all authority in heaven and on earth.

This can only mean the devil was not telling the truth. It is my firm belief that Jesus knew He had this authority when He met the devil in the wilderness. Consider these words.

Then the seventy returned with joy, saying, "Lord, even the demons are subject to us in Your name." And He said to them, "I saw Satan fall like lightning from heaven. Behold, I give you the authority to trample on serpents and scorpions, and over all the power of the enemy, and nothing shall by any means hurt you. (Luke 10:17-19 – NKJV)

At first glance, this could seem confusing. Jesus acknowledged that the devil does have some type of power. Could this be the same as the devil having authority over these kingdoms? The words used by Jesus will answer this question.

The Greek word for **authority**, which is used in the passage found in Luke 10:19, is the word exousia, which means physical and mental power; the ability or strength with which one is endued, which he either possesses or exercises.[20]

The Greek word used by the devil to express his **authority** is also the word exousia. However, the manner in which the devil used this same word has a different shade of meaning.

As I indicated previously, according to *Strong's Concordance*, this refers to his jurisdiction.[21]

This is something most would not realize by quickly reading through the devil's statements to Jesus. If you think about the entire statement the devil made, it will be evident to you. Here is the part of the statement which indicates this was only a jurisdiction.

> *All this authority I will give You, and their glory; for this*
> *has been delivered to me, and I give it to whomever I wish.*
> *(Luke 4:6 – NKJV)*

The devil readily acknowledged to Jesus that his authority was given to him and did not originate with him because of his position. The English definition of the word jurisdiction is helpful. One of several definitions of the word **jurisdiction** is: The right of a court to hear a particular case, based on the scope of its authority over the type of case and the parties to the case.[22]

The devil's only authority is the authority given to him by men and women. Even then, the scope of this authority or the jurisdiction is limited by the authority the people have to offer.

For example, I have no authority in your life unless you choose to submit to me and give me this authority. Even if you submitted to me and gave me authority over your life, I could not pass this authority on to the devil. If this sounds ridiculous or a little complicated, then consider something we often use, which is called a power of attorney. This legal document is used to transfer authority from one person to another. It allows someone else to act on your behalf.

There is no such spiritual document.

On the other hand, the concept I have just mentioned is the original basis on which the laws in the United States were written. As citizens of this great country, we have embraced a system for allowing others to act on our behalf. We are not enslaved. We are not forced to live our lives in this country. It is our choice to submit ourselves to these laws. The control system for the actions of those who act on our behalf is the power of our vote. This is the way we change who is acting on our behalf.

The ancient Jews also had an understanding of this use of the word jurisdiction, as can be seen in the following account.

And as soon as he knew that He belonged to Herod's jurisdiction, he sent Him to Herod, who was also in Jerusalem at that time. (Luke 23:7 – NKJV)

The word translated **jurisdiction**[23] in this verse is the same word translated authority in Luke 4:6. Herod did not own the part of the earth over which he had authority or jurisdiction. Neither did the devil own what he offered to Jesus.

The devil is absolutely limited to this jurisdiction. As far as humans are concerned, this is the devil's only authority. Of course, the devil will use this authority given to him by certain individuals to cause great harm to other people who have chosen to not be submitted to him.

The Greek word for **power**, used in Luke 10:19, is the word dynamis.[24] In general, the word means inherent power, or power residing in a thing by virtue of its nature, or which a person or thing exerts and puts forth.[25]

When the devil told Jesus his power had been delivered unto him, the devil admitted it was not an inherent power. Inherent power is the kind of power Jesus has. This is permanent power. It is an attribute of His character.

The power Jesus has will always be His. He has always had this power.

He spoke the worlds into existence.

Jesus knew all of this on the day the devil tempted him. The devil wasn't sure. That is, the devil did not know until these words came out of the mouth of Jesus.

> *Get behind Me, Satan! For it is written, You shall worship the LORD your God, and Him only you shall serve. (Luke 4:8 – NKJV)*

The devil realized he had a very serious problem. For years, the devil had done almost anything he pleased. Empires had risen, and empires had been overthrown. The devil ruled many evil kingdoms on this planet. This is what the devil offered to Jesus. It was not ownership, it was the evil, demonic rule over the lives of people that the devil was offering to Jesus.

> *Then the devil, taking Him up on a high mountain, showed Him all the kingdoms of the world in a moment of time. (Luke 4:5 – NKJV)*

I stated earlier that the Greek word for kingdoms refers to the territory subject to the rule of a king. The manner in which this word is used makes it clear that this is not speaking of ownership. More insight is available by looking at the word translated world.

What did the devil show Jesus that day? *Thayer* says this is the whole inhabited earth, the **world**.[26] The devil was showing Jesus the kingdoms (the part of the inhabited earth) over which he had the right to rule, or as I stated before, his jurisdiction. It had been thousands of years since the fall of man in the Garden of Eden. The devil had been constantly at work, gaining man's submission by using his tools of deception, sickness, disease, and death.

This was the authority the devil offered to Jesus. The devil would give Jesus the same right to do what the devil had been doing to the people of this earth for thousands of years.

Jesus would have none of it.

Either the devil did not know who Jesus was, or he thought Jesus did not know who He was. He may have thought Jesus did not know He already had authority. He may have thought Jesus did not know the earth already belonged to Him.

The devil failed this test
and Jesus passed it!

Jesus knew exactly who He was. He knew why He had come to this earth. Once again, I want to emphasize the purpose of this testing. It was an obvious face-to-face demonstration to the devil that Jesus knew He was the Son of God, and He knew what was ahead of Him. He came to die for our sins. Jesus was completely aware of who the devil was. He was not fooled by the devil or deceived by him like Eve was in the Garden of Eden. I don't believe it has ever been stated more clearly and eloquently than this.

He that committeth sin is of the devil; for the devil sinneth from the beginning. For this purpose the Son of God was manifested, that he might destroy the works of the devil. (1 John 3:8 – KJV)

I suspect that by this point in the encounter the devil had with Jesus, he was beginning to get the picture of what was ahead for him. This was no ordinary man. He was not like the one in the Garden of Eden. This one could not be fooled. The devil must have wondered what Jesus would do next. Why did the Son of God come to this earth?

I have covered many things in discussing this epic event in the life of Jesus. My purpose has been much more than just discussing the various aspects of an intriguing story. This is one of the events recorded in the Bible that profoundly affects us. Sadly, it has not been thought of and for the most part taught in that way.

The better we understand how completely Jesus defeated the devil in the wilderness, the more confidence we will have in the authority Jesus has delegated to us. Because of the cross and the resurrection, we have as much authority over the devil today as Jesus had when He was tempted in the wilderness.

Because of the infilling of the Holy Ghost, we now have the power that goes with this authority. This is the power promised to us as Jesus returned to Heaven.

But ye shall receive power, after that the Holy Ghost is come upon you: and ye shall be witnesses unto me both in Jerusalem, and in all Judaea, and in Samaria, and unto the uttermost part of the earth. (Acts 1:8 – KJV)

With His example in the wilderness temptation, Jesus taught us how to use this power and authority. The more we consistently use the authority we have been given over the devil, the fewer our problems will be.

Because of the death, burial, and resurrection of Jesus, the devil now knows why Jesus came to this earth. He knows he has been utterly defeated and is very aware of his ultimate end. No wonder the devil left Jesus for a more opportune time. He found out the hard way, that time would never come.

Chapter 13
A Ministry is Born

When and where did the ministry of Jesus begin? How did His ministry get started? These are essential questions, and they should be easy to answer. They are not. Did Jesus simply walk out of the wilderness after the tests had ended and begin teaching and performing miracles? It would be easy to make this assumption. But I think there is evidence that it was much more complex.

I have spent many years assisting people who desired to be teachers and preachers. It can be tough to get started. This is especially true if you are the first and only member of your family to be a minister. Thankfully, most of us had the help of an older minister when we first started to teach or preach. These senior ministers provided the opportunities needed, such as a place and a congregation who would listen and embrace us and our gifts. I know of others who began on their own. They started a church or a Bible study in their home or a friend's home.

Because I know how difficult it is to get started in the ministry, I would like to understand the beginning days of the ministry of Jesus. What kind of preparation did the Holy Spirit consider necessary? Is this something we should expect from young ministers today? Taking this approach could prove very helpful.

It may surprise you to know that there appears to be different conclusions presented by the Gospels' authors about the first few weeks of the ministry of Jesus. Since I have a firm belief in the inspiration of the Bible, I do not view these differences as contradictions. I believe each writer was filling in different details for different reasons. This is a common sense and straightforward explanation. I see no reason to think there was some kind of underlying competition or willful disagreement between the men God chose to give us this information.

Many scholars believe the ministry of Jesus began with a miracle. We know the story about Jesus turning water into wine at a wedding. But does that mean this was the beginning of His ministry? It would mean His ministry started at a wedding. That is unusual.

These ideas are due to the very different way the gospel of John begins. He provides a record of events in the ministry of Jesus that does not occur elsewhere. Some of these are found in the first few chapters of the book of John. I have heard it said that John fills in the gap of what happened in the ministry of Jesus during His first year. Perhaps. But I believe there is a more interesting way to think about these differences.

All of the Gospels contain stories of the miraculous ministry of Jesus, and all of them record some of His teachings. However, it does appear that John is more focused on the great things Jesus did, while the others are more focused on the great things Jesus said.[27] Perhaps John thought the miraculous would provide a greater appeal to those who had not yet decided to believe. When you have an opportunity, check out the "Harmony of the Gospels."

> *On the third day there was a wedding in Cana of Galilee, and the mother of Jesus was there. Now both Jesus and His disciples were invited to the wedding. And when they ran out of wine, the mother of Jesus said to Him, "They have no wine." Jesus said to her, "Woman, what does your concern have to do with Me? My hour has not yet come." His mother said to the servants, "Whatever He says to you, do it." Now there were set there six waterpots of stone, according to the manner of purification of the Jews, containing twenty or thirty gallons apiece. Jesus said to them, "Fill the waterpots with water." And they filled them up to the brim. And He said to them, "Draw some out now, and take it to the master of the feast." And they took it. When the master of the feast had tasted the water that was made wine, and did not know where it came from (but the servants who had drawn the water knew), the master of the feast called the bridegroom. And he said to him, "Every man at the beginning sets out the good wine, and when the guests have well drunk, then the inferior. You have kept the good wine until now!" This beginning of signs Jesus did in Cana of Galilee, and manifested His glory; and His disciples believed in Him. (John 2:1-11 – NKJV)*

Only John provides a record of this miracle. In his account of this miracle, John mentions this *beginning of signs Jesus did in*

149

Cana of Galilee and manifested His glory. This is a reference to the miracle. It is not a specific reference to the beginning of His ministry. John called it a sign. We can assume this means it was an indication there was a special anointing on Jesus. Instead of using the word anointing, John chose to say Jesus *manifested His glory.* But we must also keep in mind the stated purpose of the book of John. These are the words of John.

> *And many other signs truly did Jesus in the presence of His disciples, which are not written in this book. But these are written, that ye might believe that Jesus is the Christ, the Son of God, and that believing, ye might have life through His name. (John 20:30-31 – KJ21)*

John desired his readers to be aware of the manifestation of the glory that resided in Jesus. The proof of this glory was the sign. I do not think John intended this to mean the first evidence of this manifested glory was synonymous with the beginning of the ministry of Jesus.

The assumption has been made that the ministry of Jesus did not begin until He started performing miracles. I do understand this perspective. This would certainly draw a crowd. Typically, it would also create anticipation that other miracles would happen. But I am not convinced this is how Jesus wanted to begin His ministry. I do not question that Jesus wanted to help people who were hurting or in need of His help. However, my view is that His primary focus was teaching.

Having the ability to perform miracles set Jesus apart from the other teachers. But was this the major reason Jesus came to earth? Or was the message Jesus brought more significant?

Can we even make this distinction? Perhaps it isn't necessary to determine this since He did both very well.

If we are to assume the ministry of Jesus began with performing a miracle, and this is the indication a person should be in the ministry, we have a severe problem. I believe a person must be filled with the Holy Spirit to be adequately prepared for the ministry. This does not mean a person is ready to turn water into wine. The church's history is replete with information about very influential ministers who did not have miracles in their services. This may have been a possibility they knew nothing about. We must always remember that the knowledge of the supernatural was something Jesus knew more about than we ever will know. His birth was supernatural. A complete understanding of the miraculous is not essential to the beginning stages of a ministry. But something else is necessary.

At the end of the same verse, it says, *and His disciples believed in Him.* Jesus had disciples. This must be considered.

This is an indication the ministry of Jesus had already begun.

Having spent years in the ministry, I can state that gaining committed followers is the hardest part. It should also be clear a ministry can't exist long without these committed followers. We must have the help of many precious people to accomplish our assigned tasks. It is all about building trust.

I have stated more than once we do not have a factual chronology of the life and ministry of Jesus in the Gospels. The Holy Ghost did not think this was necessary or important.

The message is far more critical than the sequence of events. My conclusion is that the beginning of the ministry of Jesus was a process. It took place in several different and seemingly unconnected places, events, and times. This miracle of turning water into wine does appear to be the first miracle performed by Jesus. It is proper to conclude it was **one of the beginning events** in the ministry of Jesus. However, what happened in the synagogue may have been much more critical.

Performing a miracle by getting a group of men to do what you ask them to do is no small feat. The Holy Spirit was at work in the life of Jesus. However, Jesus said nothing to indicate there would be more miracles. No blind eyes were opened at the wedding. No broken hearts were mended. No lives were changed forever.

The transition from the Holy Ghost doing things to Jesus and for Jesus, to working through Him for the benefit of others had begun. I do not question this. However, I am inclined to mark the beginning of the ministry of Jesus with His teaching. Jesus spent much of His time teaching. Many people only want to see miracles or to receive healing. While these things are necessary, they do not have an eternal impact. Bringing the message of eternal life was the reason Jesus came to earth.

What happened in the synagogue can be viewed as a significant time of transition for Jesus. In those few moments, everything changed. His water baptism, His experience in the wilderness temptation, beginning to teach, heal the sick, and do miracles came together in this one epic moment. In the great wisdom of God, the Holy Ghost was always at work, causing things to happen in the life of Jesus. These experiences were to help Him grow in wisdom, maturity, and favor with God and man. **God had never been a man.** He had never lived in a human body. But in Jesus, this was the task at hand. What would it be like for God to live through a man? The Holy Ghost was never at a loss in dealing with this question.

It appears this event in the synagogue took place just a few weeks after Jesus came out of the wilderness. The only time frame given is that Jesus had been traveling and teaching. As a result, He had become very popular. I am sure Jesus was a welcome relief from what the people had endured every Sabbath day. There had been no good news at the synagogue for four hundred years. This young man was full of life and hope. He was saying things the other speakers never spoke about. When Luke began to share the story of the wilderness temptation, he opened his account with these words.

> *Then Jesus, being filled with the Holy Spirit, returned from the Jordan and was led by the Spirit into the wilderness. (Luke 4:1 – NKJV)*

The synagogue event began with the same message.

> *And Jesus returned in the power of the Spirit into Galilee. (Luke 4:14 – KJV)*

Luke desired to convey the influence of the Holy Spirit in the life of Jesus as He went through both of these experiences. Luke was convinced of the Holy Spirit's effect on the life and ministry of Jesus. I am also confident of the influence of the Holy Spirit on the life of Jesus. The Holy Spirit was at work in the life of Jesus, developing Him into the man He became.

The ministry of Jesus had eternal consequences. It also would have a significant impact on millions of people while they lived on Earth. The Holy Spirit was well aware of every aspect of this short time of ministry and its great importance.

The trip to the synagogue began as it had in the past. There was nothing out of the ordinary about the service. But without warning to the public, the Holy Ghost took the next step. How quickly the hearts and minds of the people were revealed.

The verses Jesus chose to read that day were a great window into the ministry of Jesus. The people suddenly realized Jesus was talking about what He had been doing and what He was going to do. Yet, not much detail is given regarding how He would do these things.

> *And Jesus returned in the power of the Spirit into Galilee: and there went out a fame of him through all the region round about. And he taught in their synagogues, being glorified of all. And he came to Nazareth, where he had been brought up: and, as his custom was, he went into the synagogue on the sabbath day, and stood up for to read. And there was delivered unto him the book of the prophet Esaias. And when he had opened the book, he found the place where it was written, The Spirit of the Lord is upon me, because he hath anointed me to preach the gospel to the poor; he hath sent me to heal the brokenhearted, to preach deliverance to the captives, and recovering of sight to the blind, to set at liberty them that are bruised, To preach the acceptable year of the Lord. And he closed the book, and he gave it again to the minister, and sat*

down. And the eyes of all them that were in the synagogue were fastened on him. And he began to say unto them, This day is this scripture fulfilled in your ears. (Luke 4:14-21 – KJV)

Nothing happened in the wilderness temptation to weaken or diminish the presence and the power of the Holy Spirit in Jesus. This is our example. We go through many things in life which are challenging. Yet, the plan of God is for us to come out of each experience as vital, if not stronger than we were when it began. This is possible. I am reminded of something I read years ago about the following verse.

But Jesus looked at them and said to them, "With men this is impossible, but with God all things are possible." (Matthew 19:26 – NKJV)

A wise minister commented on this verse and made a profound and enlightening remark. He said, "God never said everything would be easy. He said it would be possible."

The experience Jesus had in the wilderness was not easy. Putting up with the devil harassing us for a few minutes is not easy. This is why we are told to resist him. This is why we should always have on the armor of God. Winning some of these fights can be challenging. The good news is that we can win. It is possible. Jesus won this battle in the wilderness, and look at the result.

Matthew explains that John the Baptist had been put in prison, so Jesus chose to move from Nazareth to Galilee. This was a wise decision. Jesus began to assemble His team. He chose Simon, called Peter, and Andrew, his brother. Next,

Jesus chose James, the son of Zebedee, and John, his brother. These appear to be the first four of the twelve disciples. Then we have something extraordinary.

> *And Jesus went about all Galilee, teaching in their synagogues, preaching the gospel of the kingdom, and healing all kinds of sickness and all kinds of disease among the people. Then His fame went throughout all Syria; and they brought to Him all sick people who were afflicted with various diseases and torments, and those who were demon-possessed, epileptics, and paralytics; and He healed them. Great multitudes followed Him—from Galilee, and from Decapolis, Jerusalem, Judea, and beyond the Jordan. (Matthew 4:23-25 – NKJV)*

Wow! This is the way things should be. This is the will of God. This is the work of the Holy Ghost in the life of Jesus. Some prominent ministers have clearly stated that this type of ministry is not available today. They will quickly add that God still does heal people today but want to believe it does not happen through us as it did through Jesus. I could not disagree more. This is the same as saying Jesus was not our example for ministry. If this is true, then who is our model? Whom do we emulate? Is it some person without the power of the Holy Ghost? I think not!

Jesus did these things, like healing the sick and casting out devils, because the people needed it so badly. He also did these incredible healings and performed these miracles to show us it can be done. Jesus was and is our example of ministry. I desire to only be like Him. We will see more of these healings, signs, and wonders in the future. Everything Jesus did is needed today. No matter where you live, there are people in great need. We have a great God, and He desires to do these same things through us. This is why we have the Holy Ghost.

> *Having concluded these great meetings, Jesus came to Nazareth, where he had been brought up: and, as his custom was, he went into the synagogue on the sabbath day, and stood up for to read. (Luke 4:16 – KJV)*

What was Jesus expecting?
How much did He know?

These were His people. His family and friends were there. They attended this synagogue. Jesus had come home, and I feel sure He wanted to do the same things for them He had been doing in Galilee. The needs were there, and Jesus was filled with the power of the Spirit. To put it mildly, the reaction of the hometown crowd was not positive. I will share that part later. It is shocking.

The next section of this story is comprised of the reading from the Book of Isaiah. I have included the *King James Version* of the passage from Isaiah for comparison.

> *The Spirit of the Lord GOD is upon me; because the LORD hath anointed me to preach good tidings unto the meek; he hath sent me to bind up the brokenhearted, to proclaim liberty to the captives, and the opening of the prison to them that are bound; To proclaim the acceptable year of the LORD, and the day of vengeance of our God; to comfort all that mourn; To appoint unto them that mourn in Zion, to give unto them beauty for ashes, the oil*

> *of joy for mourning, the garment of praise for the spirit of heaviness; that they might be called trees of righteousness, the planting of the LORD, that he might be glorified. (Isaiah 61:1-3 – KJV)*

Earlier in this chapter I included this passage (as we find it) in the Gospel of Luke. Jesus did not quote this scripture passage exactly the way it is written in our Bibles in the book of Isaiah. What Jesus said includes six distinctly different assignments which became the earmarks of His ministry. They are as follows:

To preach the gospel to the poor.

To heal the brokenhearted.

To preach deliverance to the captives.

To bring recovering of sight to the blind.

To set at liberty them that are bruised.

To preach the acceptable year of the Lord.

I call these the "Six Facets of a Holy Ghost Ministry." This should be a list of the things happening in Spirit-filled churches. Otherwise, I am not sure they should be called Spirit-filled churches. The day is coming when these things will happen in every place, where Spirit-filled believers gather. These will be six of the earmarks of the next Great Awakening. Therefore, every person in the ministry must anticipate the opportunities for these things to occur as they follow the direction of the Holy Ghost. We won't do this unless we believe it is possible. Everything about ministry revolves around our faith in our relationship with God.

We must not only have faith to receive the Holy Ghost; we must have confidence that the Holy Ghost will work through us as He worked through Jesus.

Without taking time for an extensive analysis, one significant difference stands out when comparing the scriptures in Isaiah with those in Luke. This is the shocking absence of any reference to healing in the prophecy given by Isaiah. There is no mention of recovering sight for the blind or any other disease, deformity, or sickness. This says more about Jesus and the Holy Ghost than Isaiah. The Prophet was only expressing what God had given him to say. He did his job well.

We do not know if the original text included any mention of healing. We don't have any originals to examine. The assumption must be made that this was not part of the prophecy. We know comments about healing would not have been inconsistent with other statements in the book of Isaiah. The prophet Isaiah gave us excellent information about Jesus hundreds of years before His birth. Then he spoke emphatically of the provision Jesus made for our healing.

> *But he was wounded for our transgressions, he was bruised for our iniquities: the chastisement of our peace was upon him; and with his stripes we are healed. (Isaiah 53:5 – KJV)*

We cannot resolve this difference any further between what Isaiah prophesied and what is recorded in the New Testament. So, let's consider the perspective Jesus had that day as He read from the book of Isaiah. Remember, Jesus had just come from Galilee and the surrounding area. He had experienced tremendous success. No other person in history has yet done what Jesus did in this one series of meetings. That is a critical assessment.

You can take my last statement in one of two ways. It can be seen as a criticism, which is not my intention. Or, you can view this as something exciting for the future. Jesus said we would do the same things He did and even greater things than these. I have experienced this to a certain degree. I have seen blind eyes open and have touched those who were deaf, and they could then hear. But I am not satisfied that I have accomplished all the Holy Ghost has empowered me to do. I long for there to be more demonstrations of God's glory. And it will happen. I expect to be a part of this for the remainder of my life.

I invite you to do as I have done. I took the list of six things I gave you from the passage Jesus read in the synagogue and compared it to the report given by Matthew. Every experience on that list can be found in the account of the first meetings Jesus conducted. In one respect, this is remarkable. Yet, in another, it is precisely what we should expect. If you did not know what I just told you, consider what this means after you recover from the surprise.

When Jesus was reading from the Book of Isaiah, He was not thinking about what might happen someday. I am confident Jesus was reliving what He had just seen as He was ministering to the people. Jesus was living what Isaiah prophesied. No doubt Jesus knew how God was fulfilling what the prophets had said about Him. We must think like Jesus. We are also living what has been prophesied. It is time for us to get out of the someday mentality and expect what Jesus said about us to be fulfilled.

We can do the same things Jesus did.

I will talk about these six facets of ministry a little later in this book. But right now, let's return to the beginning words of this passage Jesus read from the book of Isaiah and take this one step at a time. Jesus began with these words. *The Spirit of the Lord is upon me.* Every person in the synagogue was looking at Jesus. They did not do this because it was a respectful thing for them to do. Word had traveled fast, and many stories were circulating about Jesus. No doubt they were all wondering what was going to happen next.

It was their custom to have some person read a passage from the Old Covenant when they met in the synagogue. Some person familiar with the scrolls would hand the requested book to the reader. Then it was up to the reader to find the desired passage. This is what Jesus did. Why did Jesus choose these words? Did He want to communicate something to His friends and family? I am convinced He did.

Many of those in attendance had heard the stories about the miracles. Blind people talk when they receive their sight. Lepers are excited to be back with their families. People who have been paralyzed go everywhere they can to show people what God has done. The story of the water baptism had also been repeated many times.

There was probably a lot of talk about the dove-like creature and especially the voice that spoke from heaven. The Jews had a historical perspective of God interacting with them. But it had been hundreds of years since anything had happened. Thoughts of what this meant must have swirled through their minds as they looked at this man called Jesus. There was something different about Him.

When Jesus read those words, *The Spirit of the Lord is upon me*, did He mean to say this was talking about Him? We know He did, but did they know it? I often wonder what they thought this meant.

> Perhaps you recall John the Baptist said: *I indeed baptize you with water unto repentance. but he that cometh after me is mightier than I, whose shoes I am not worthy to bear: he shall baptize you with the Holy Ghost, and with fire: (Matthew 3:11 – KJV)*

Is it correct for those baptized with the Holy Ghost to include themselves in this declaration? Jesus was declaring: *The Spirit of the Lord is upon me*. We should be stating the same thing. The Spirit of the Lord is upon me. Are you this bold? You should be. You have the same Holy Ghost Jesus had when He stood in the synagogue. You and I have the same power. Why not make it obvious that we believe we have the ability Jesus promised we would have when we received the Holy Spirit?

Jesus has baptized us with what He has!

The reason for the Spirit of the Lord being on Jesus is stated with great clarity. It was because the Holy Ghost had anointed Him. In this short statement, we have two keys to a successful ministry. Those two keys are "the Spirit of the Lord" and "the anointing." These can't be separated. Where you find one, you have the potential for the other.

If the Spirit of the Lord is not on a person, then that person is not anointed. If a person is not anointed, that person does not have the Spirit of the Lord on them. There are many people in places of ministry who have neither. They speak eloquently, but there is no power. They may scream and make lots of noise, but there are no results. They are dignified, but nothing changes in people's lives. The power of persuasion is not the anointing. Having lots of money and millions of followers are not evidence of the anointing or the presence of the Spirit of the Lord.

At some point during the days Jesus spent in the wilderness, His cousin John the Baptist was arrested and put in prison.

> *Now when Jesus had heard that John was cast into prison, he departed into Galilee. (Matthew 4:12 – KJV)*

We are not told how much time passed after John was arrested until He sent a message to Jesus, but it was long enough for Jesus to choose the twelve disciples and begin training them. John the Baptist had been in prison all this time. I don't think he spoke out of discouragement. I believe he just wanted to ensure he had accomplished his mission in life. John had boldly declared Jesus to be the one God was sending to the world. However, John needed to be reassured.

> *Now when John had heard in the prison the works of Christ, he sent two of his disciples, And said unto him, Art thou he that should come, or do we look for another? Jesus answered and said unto them, Go and shew John again those things which ye do hear and see: The*

> *blind receive their sight, and the lame walk, the lepers are cleansed, and the deaf hear, the dead are raised up, and the poor have the gospel preached to them. (Matthew 11:2-5 – KJV)*

If the timing of these events in the life of John the Baptist and Jesus was as it appears in the Bible, then John was not in the meetings in and around Galilee. John had not seen the Spirit of the Lord on Jesus since the day he baptized Him in water. There had been no opportunity for John to experience the anointing on Jesus. John had heard many of the stories. I find this interesting. The man was in prison, and he was not popular with those who incarcerated him. John was on death row. Interestingly enough, two of John's disciples had access to him in prison and had told him many things.

But John wanted a personal word from Jesus.

It is always exciting to hear what God has done for other people. We are glad for them, and we rejoice with them. However, no matter who we are or how strong we are, we all want to hear from God. Nothing comes close to the value and the meaning of a direct word from God. The good news is that God is eager to speak into our lives. Sometimes this will be direct. At other times, God will communicate with us through another person. God has given us several gifts of the Spirit, which the Holy Ghost uses to fulfill this desire to hear from God. In later books, we will closely examine all of those gifts.

The response Jesus sent back to John speaks volumes. Jesus said: *Go and shew John again those things which ye do hear and see: The blind receive their sight, and the lame walk, the lepers are cleansed, and the deaf hear, the dead are raised up, and the poor have the gospel preached to them.* Jesus said to show these things to John again. The Greek word for **shew** used in this Scripture is a word that means to bring tidings (from a person or thing), bring word, or a report.[28]

The disciples of John were to tell John what Jesus said. The intriguing part was what Jesus wanted John to know. The report from Jesus to John recounted many things Isaiah had prophesied about Jesus. Isn't it interesting that Jesus began His proof statement of who He was with the words: *The blind receive their sight.* Jesus concluded His message with another reference to what He had read in the synagogue: *The poor have the gospel preached to them.*

John believed in Jesus, and Jesus knew it. Jesus also believed in John. Jesus did not hesitate to send His cousin solid proof of who He was. Jesus was not insulted or offended that John had asked for evidence.

Jesus will prove himself to you as well.

The Holy Ghost anointed Jesus to do all those things. This may seem odd to say it in that way. It is just another way of expressing the original statement. *The Spirit of the Lord is upon me, because he hath anointed me.* The same thing can be said of us. Spirit-filled believers need to understand this. The Holy Ghost has anointed us to do what we have been assigned to do.

Anyone who does anything worthwhile will be able to do it only because the Holy Ghost has anointed them. Most, but not all, of what Jesus did in His ministry – He did through the gifts of the Spirit spoken of in the book of 1 Corinthians. However, there were those times when God did things in the life of Jesus which will never be repeated. An excellent example is the story of the transfiguration of Jesus.

> *Now after six days Jesus took Peter, James, and John his brother, led them up on a high mountain by themselves; and He was transfigured before them. His face shone like the sun, and His clothes became as white as the light. And behold, Moses and Elijah appeared to them, talking with Him. Then Peter answered and said to Jesus, "Lord, it is good for us to be here; if You wish, let us make here three tabernacles: one for You, one for Moses, and one for Elijah." While he was still speaking, behold, a bright cloud overshadowed them; and suddenly a voice came out of the cloud, saying, "This is My beloved Son, in whom I am well pleased. Hear Him!" And when the disciples heard it, they fell on their faces and were greatly afraid. But Jesus came and touched them and said, "Arise, and do not be afraid." When they had lifted up their eyes, they saw no one but Jesus only. Now as they came down from the mountain, Jesus commanded them, saying, "Tell the vision to no one until the Son of Man is risen from the dead." (Matthew 17:1-9 – NKJV)*

Over the many years I have been in the ministry, I have boldly declared that every believer should be doing the works Jesus did. I have explained that this is possible because of the Holy Ghost and His gifts. Invariably some person will confront me with one of the events, such as the one above, as their excuse for not doing what Jesus said we could do.

I aim to clarify that certain things happened to Jesus, such as the transfiguration event, which we will never experience. If you ever wonder about something you are attempting to do and want to know if the Holy Ghost has empowered you to do it, there is a way to find out. All that is necessary is to answer three questions. Did Jesus ever do what you are attempting to do? If Jesus did not do it, but it is spoken of in the Bible, then who caused it to happen? Did the event originate in heaven or on this earth? The answers can be found in the Bible.

The transfiguration of Jesus will never happen again. The water baptism of Jesus will never happen again. It is only in these two events where it is recorded that a voice spoke from Heaven and said: *This is My beloved Son, in whom I am well pleased. Hear Him!* Jesus did not do these things. They happened to Him. He did not do them. They originated in heaven because **God the Father caused them to happen**. After the transfiguration had ended, Jesus swore them to secrecy until after His resurrection.

Jesus never anticipated
we would be doing things His Father did.

No matter how powerfully God uses you in the anointing He has bestowed upon you, you can do nothing to cause a voice to speak from heaven. You will never use one of the gifts of the Spirit to cause a dove-like creature to descend from heaven. It is better to be busy doing what we have been instructed to do, like laying hands on the sick, than to be concerned about things we can't do. Why have I gone to such lengths to explain this?

The anointing on Jesus is the same anointing on you and me. The same Spirit of the Lord is on us. Our responsibility is to do the same things Jesus did, so we must be clear about what is included and what is not.

If you check *Strong's Concordance* and look at the meanings given for the Greek word translated **anoint**, you will discover the following information.

To **anoint** means: a. Consecrating Jesus to the Messianic office and furnishing him with the necessary powers for its administration. b. **Enduing Christians with the gifts of the Holy Spirit.**[29] Finding such statements in *Strong's Concordance* *is* rare. This got my attention. Immediately another verse of Scripture came to mind.

> *Behold, I send the Promise of My Father upon you; but tarry in the city of Jerusalem until you are endued with power from on high." (Luke 24:49 – NKJV)*

The Greek word in this verse, which has been translated as **endued**, is a different word from the one used to express the concepts of the anointing. This Greek word means to put on or to clothe oneself.[30] The message from Jesus to the people that He told to wait in Jerusalem for the outpouring of the Holy Ghost was clear. They would put on something, or be clothed with something which they did not previously have. Power from on high would be theirs. They would become witnesses to the World of the great things Jesus had done.

I have always wondered how they felt about Jesus telling them to go into all the World and preach the Gospel. One thing is certain, all of this required their cooperation.

Once again, I will point out that the word endued means to clothe oneself. The Holy Ghost will not force Himself on you. You make the decision to be clothed with the Holy Spirit.

Endued is not a word we use every day. It means to endow or provide with a quality or ability.[31] Jesus was telling His disciples; you will have the same ability I have when you are filled with the Holy Ghost. And it will be the same quality. This is our endowment, and it is more precious than gold.

The Spirit of the Lord is upon us because He has anointed us. He has endued us with power from on high. We have received our endowment. We have the ability to do what Jesus did, and it will be of the same quality.

Chapter 14
Preach the Word

Do you believe you can do the things Jesus did while He was here on earth? This might seem like a ridiculous question if Jesus had not said what He did. He has great faith in the abilities He gave to us. It is exciting to think of the possibilities this may provide. I have discovered that only a few people believe we can do these things. I am one of the few. I have embraced this as my assignment. I trust you have done the same.

> *Most assuredly, I say to you, he who believes in Me, the works that I do he will do also; and greater works than these he will do, because I go to My Father. (John 14:12 – NKJV)*

In this chapter, I want to consider these statements from another perspective. Your reaction to this Scripture depends almost entirely on what you have been taught about Jesus and our relationship with Him. Down through the ages, these words from Jesus recorded by John have troubled, amazed, confounded, and excited many Christians. I have done my best to present Jesus in the pages of this book as we see Him in the Bible. Jesus was the Son of God. He still is. Jesus was also a man. He still is. This may not be completely understood until we see Him face-to-face. We accept this by faith and proceed to do what Jesus taught us.

It is safe to say most Christians think of Jesus as God and almost not human at all. They can accept the idea that baby Jesus was human. But when we begin to discuss the stories of Jesus healing the sick, performing miracles, and raising the dead, it is hard for them to see Jesus as a man. The thought of doing something Jesus did, such as incredibly miraculous things, is more than many are ready to accept.

If Jesus could heal the sick only because He was God, why did He tell us to lay hands on the sick? We are not gods. Jesus knew this. Why would Jesus ask us to do something we can't do? For that matter, if Jesus was healing sick people because He was God, why did He make these statements to his disciples?

> *And when he had called unto him his twelve disciples, he gave them power against unclean spirits, to cast them out, and to heal all manner of sickness and all manner of disease. Now the names of the twelve apostles are these; The first, Simon, who is called Peter, and Andrew his brother; James the son of Zebedee, and John his brother; Philip, and Bartholomew; Thomas, and Matthew the publican; James the son of Alphaeus, and Lebbaeus, whose surname was Thaddaeus; Simon the Canaanite, and Judas Iscariot, who also betrayed him. These twelve Jesus sent forth, and commanded them, saying, Go not into the way of the Gentiles, and into any city of the*

Samaritans enter ye not: But go rather to the lost sheep of the house of Israel. And as ye go, preach, saying, The kingdom of heaven is at hand. Heal the sick, cleanse the lepers, raise the dead, cast out devils: freely ye have received, freely give. (Matthew 10:1-8 – KJV)

We have a dilemma. If Jesus was healing people because He was God, then at least for a time, He turned these twelve men into gods. The very idea Jesus would do such a thing is ludicrous. To do such a thing would be completely contradictory to His character. We know Jesus did not turn them into gods. At no point in time were any of these men gods. One of these men lied; one was full of doubt, and another committed suicide. These men were human. Yet, Jesus told them to heal the sick. Jesus told them to heal all manner of sickness and disease.

Despite their shortcomings and their humanness, these men did do the same things Jesus had been doing. We know they did because they reported it back to Jesus. And we have a record of it in the Bible. Moreover, once they were filled with the Holy Ghost, they proceeded to do even more of the things Jesus had done.

Some have argued that these men could do these things because they were disciples. The argument goes that when these men died, the whole idea of healing the sick became moot. Then why doesn't the Bible say this? Why didn't Jesus make this clear in His teaching? This would have been valuable information for the early church to have. If this is true, then why are we left to think the things Jesus said apply to us, just as they applied to the disciples?

These twelve men were with Jesus every day. They knew Jesus personally and talked to Him all the time. If healing the sick ceased to be possible when all twelve of these men died, what does this say about the apostle Paul? Most Christians are willing to include Paul in the group, who could do miraculous things. But they are unwilling to go any further. They are only shortchanging themselves. Hundreds of thousands of people have been healed by the laying on of hands. I desire to see more people healed of even more sicknesses and diseases.

We have the tools we need to do this job. What we need is a better understanding of how to use these tools. I refer to the nine gifts of the Holy Spirit listed in 1 Corinthians chapter 12. Because of this lack of understanding, proficiency in the function of these gifts is seriously lacking. Many people who have received the Holy Spirit seem to fear being used by God in any of these gifts. This is a timidity we must shed.

Now concerning spiritual gifts, brethren, I would not have you ignorant. Ye know that ye were Gentiles, carried away unto these dumb idols, even as ye were led. Wherefore I give you to understand, that no man speaking by the Spirit of God calleth Jesus accursed: and that no man can say that Jesus is the Lord but by the Holy Ghost. Now there are diversities of gifts, but the same Spirit. And there are differences of administrations, but the same Lord. And there are diversities of operations, but it is the same God which worketh all in all. But the manifestation of the Spirit is given to every man to profit withal. For to one is given by the Spirit the word of wisdom; to another the word of knowledge by the same

Spirit; To another faith by the same Spirit; to another the gifts of healing by the same Spirit; To another the working of miracles; to another prophecy; to another discerning of spirits; to another divers kinds of tongues; to another the interpretation of tongues: But all these worketh that one and the selfsame Spirit, dividing to every man severally as he will. (1 Corinthians 12:1-11 – KJV)

Men and women of God have preferred to argue about the meaning of these words rather than accept them as truth. Some will even attempt to argue over the word gifts. I know other translations alter some of this wording. But you can't change the concepts embodied in it. Some ministers refuse to call the nine things listed in the verses above gifts of the Spirit. This objection is based on the first four words of verse one.

The word gifts can't be found in some Greek texts. This has been used to say these are the Spirit's manifestations. They claim these are not gifts we have received. I have several questions. If these are not gifts the Holy Spirit wants us to have, why did Paul call them *gifts* in verse four? Why did Paul say *the manifestation of the Spirit is given to every man* in verse seven? Why did Paul use the words *For to one is given by the Spirit* in verse eight? These are gifts of the Spirit. More importantly, if these *gifts* are not intended for us, it is impossible to explain this verse.

But covet earnestly the best gifts: and yet shew I unto you a more excellent way. (1 Corinthians 12:31 – KJV)

While people have been suffering and dying of every horrible sickness and disease known to man, the religious theologians have discussed and argued. It is time to embrace what the Holy Ghost has made available. It is time to do the works Jesus did and even greater works. Can you imagine what will happen one of these days soon when the Holy Ghost is poured out upon all flesh? There will be people worldwide who understand and walk in the fullness of what I have been explaining in the paragraphs of this chapter. I am eager to see this day come.

If the only Scripture I knew from the Bible was the one that says Jesus said I could do the works He did, I would want to find out how He did those works. This would be my first reaction. I would immediately resolve to discover the answer. Then if I read the passage from 1 Corinthians about the gifts of the Spirit, I would think this might be the answer. My next logical step would be to find out if this was correct. I do not understand why most Christians do not seem to think this way. I do think this way. Thus, I have researched this thoroughly to share it with you.

For many years, it has been common to divide these nine things listed in 1 Corinthians 12, which I have called gifts of the Spirit, into three groups. You will discover this in most of the books that have been published on the topic of the Holy Spirit. It is commonly accepted as fact, so I will consider it as such for our purposes.

These three groupings are then used to encompass the nine gifts into groups of three gifts each. In his book, *The Gifts and Ministries of the Holy Spirit*, Lester Sumrall has stated that these three groupings are as follows. Group one is the Revelation Gifts consisting of the word of wisdom, the word of knowledge, and discerning of spirits. Group two is the Power Gifts consisting of the gift of faith, the gifts of healing, and the working of miracles. Group three is the Inspiration Gifts consisting of the gift of prophecy, the gift of tongues, and the interpretation of tongues.[32]

This information has resonated with millions of people to such a degree that most have not searched for more truth. In concept, I agree. However, I believe there is much more to know. Without meaning to take anything away from what Lester Sumrall has said, I believe this is only the place to begin. Because of the discussion which follows in his book, it is obvious Sumrall was of the same opinion. He has done an excellent job expounding on the meaning and purpose of these gifts. I am concerned that some may have limited their understanding considerably by clinging too tightly to this specific way of thinking about these nine gifts of the Spirit.

I would like to refer back to the passage in Luke where it is recorded that Jesus read from the book of Isaiah.

> *The Spirit of the Lord is upon me, because he hath anointed me to preach the gospel to the poor; he hath sent me to heal the brokenhearted, to preach deliverance to the captives, and recovering of sight to the blind, to set at liberty them that are bruised, To preach the acceptable year of the Lord. (Luke 4:18-19 – KJV)*

As I indicated in the previous chapter, we can easily break these two verses down into a list of six significant statements. Those six statements are that we must preach the gospel to the poor. Heal the broken-hearted. Preach deliverance to the captives. (Preach) recovering of sight to the blind. Set at liberty them that are bruised. Preach the acceptable year of the Lord.

Considering our list, we can do at least two exciting and informative things with it. First we must take into account that seven of the nine gifts of the Spirit can be identified in this list from the book of Luke. The two missing gifts are diverse kinds of tongues and the interpretation of tongues.

The second is to realize that almost everything Jesus did fits into one of these six categories. I will provide examples. However, I must say it was never the plan of God for these things to stop with the return of the Lord Jesus to heaven.

Jesus intended for us to continue to do the things He was doing.

As I study the Bible, I can't find any place where there is a record of Jesus ministering to people without the assistance of the Holy Spirit. God help us to be so wise. Those who speak in tongues regularly tend to think of these vocal gifts first when ministering to people. Consider how much Jesus did with no record of Him ever speaking in tongues. This is not to say we should speak in tongues less. No. We should function in these other gifts more.

The operation of these seven gifts of the Spirit defines the anointing that was on Jesus. Remember, the passage He read from Isaiah begins with the words, *The Spirit of the Lord is upon me because He has anointed me.* Without question, this list of six things is what Jesus was called to do.

We should never minister without at least some of these nine gifts of the Spirit operating while we minister.

If my challenge seems a bit radical, consider the alternative. What is happening if we minister (or attempt to minister) without the aid of any of these gifts? Does this not mean we are only trying to accomplish something in our power and natural wisdom? Does this not become much ado about nothing?

In a world as complex as ours, even the smartest are floundering. We have challenges for which no person has answers. Our brightest medical minds are constantly at a loss for solutions to new and more horrible diseases. Men can invent things they can't control. Politics is so filled with lies that there is no trust. This may sound very depressing, but it makes the point. Words of wisdom and words of knowledge are things we can no longer live without. Gifts of healings and miracles are a must. If those who minister don't have these gifts, who will?

To explain my comments about this list of six things as they apply to the ministry of Jesus, it is essential to eliminate a few things. First, it should be clear that I am not limiting the entire ministry of Jesus to this list. He did many things that were not included on the list. Jesus was crucified and buried. After three days, Jesus rose from the dead. These things are not included in the list. When Jesus rose from the dead, He had a human body, but it was not the same as ours. Again, this is not on the list.

This new human body Jesus had after the resurrection could do things our human bodies cannot do. It is fascinating to read about Jesus appearing in rooms where the doors were locked, then disappearing at will. The anointing on Jesus as He sat in the synagogue was not for this purpose. I do not see the need to belabor the point further except to clarify one thing.

The anointing on Jesus was for a specific purpose. This purpose had nothing to do with providing a personal benefit to Jesus. The benefactors were the people Jesus saw and touched. When we become this focused on allowing the Holy Spirit to work through us in similar ways to benefit those in need, we will experience the same results.

It saddens me to see so much focus by ministers on their own needs and desires. This has never been the purpose of ministry. I must have confidence that God will meet my needs. He will see that my family and I are taken care of. This does not mean I subject my family to unnecessary difficulties. It does not mean I must suffer for my zeal. Enough suffering accompanies the ministry without purposely creating any. I have never understood why there seems to be such a drawing to these extremes.

Like Jesus said when He was only twelve years old, I must be about my Father's business. And if that business encompasses the list I have shown you from the book of Luke, then my ministry will have incorporated many of the works of Jesus. We will look more deeply at these things. We may begin to envision how even more incredible things are possible.

The first item on the list is to preach the gospel to the poor. Perhaps you noticed the word *preach* appears or is implied four times in this list. Before I describe what is included in preaching the gospel to the poor, we must consider what gifts of the Spirit should be involved in this part of the assignment. Too much preaching relies entirely on the skill and intellect of the preacher. I am not opposed to being skilled at doing our job; gifting is essential and Biblical.

However, nothing can replace the anointing.

Sadly, this anointing has never been defined in the hearts and minds of many who preach. It is too connected to emotion or the ability to sway the crowd. Many great orators can impress a group of people and move them to tears or laughter. Some can even seem to do this at will. But any person who has experienced the anointing knows full well when the anointing is not present. Just what do we mean by the use of the word anointing? In essence, this is what I have set out to describe.

One of the best ways to think of the anointing is to consider the results of its presence. **The anointing makes things happen that would never happen if it were not present and active.** Consider this in the light of the gifts of the Spirit. I will refer you to the information we gleaned from Lester Sumrall. He listed three of the gifts of the Spirit under the heading of the Revelation Gifts. According to Sumrall, the gifts of revelation are the word of wisdom, the word of knowledge, and the discerning of Spirits.[33]

Without expounding on the meaning of each of these gifts, it should be easy to assume these things would be good if they were included in all preaching. Why would we not want there to be wisdom, knowledge, and discernment in what we preach? Granted, I am not even scratching the surface of what these gifts are all about.

If the Holy Spirit provided some of these gifts to reveal things we would not otherwise know, they belong in our preaching. For the moment, allow this to be a limited definition of what it means to be anointed. I will state it more clearly. The anointing is the assistance of the Holy Spirit in revealing things I don't know as I preach. I would not say or even think of these things without this assistance. To make our definition richer, consider the substance of the revelation. The anointing of the Holy Spirit provides me with wisdom I did not have when I prepared my sermon. This same anointing provides the knowledge I did not get from my study time and the ability to discern how my audience receives what I have to say.

This may be entirely new for you. I know it will be to some. For others, I am putting into words something you have enjoyed, appreciated, and your audiences have benefited from many times. Maybe this will help you express what has been occurring a little better. Even more so, I hope you will find these words beneficial as you allow these precious gifts to work in your life as you preach. Consider the topics mentioned by Isaiah and addressed by Jesus.

We are to preach to the poor. We are to preach to the captives. We are to preach to the blind. We are to preach the acceptable year of the Lord. All of these certainly require more wisdom and knowledge than I have. This is why I have said anointed preaching and teaching must and it will include all three of the gifts of Revelation.

What would be an example of Jesus preaching the gospel to the poor? To answer this question, I must introduce another essential facet of preaching. It is never just about words. Actual preaching includes action. It provokes action in the preacher and encourages activity in those who hear the preaching. If this does not happen, there will be no lasting results. Two incredible stories illustrate this first item on our list. I will briefly discuss only one because they are similar. Also, the first miracle I will discuss is the feeding of the five thousand. This is the only miracle performed by Jesus, which was included in all four of the Gospels. All of the accounts contain the same basic information, so I have chosen the story as it appears in the gospel of Mark.

> *And Jesus, when he came out, saw much people, and was moved with compassion toward them, because they were as sheep not having a shepherd: and he began to teach them many things. And when the day was now far spent, his disciples came unto him, and said, This is a desert place, and now the time is far passed: Send them away, that they may go into the country round about, and into the villages, and buy themselves bread: for they have nothing to eat. He answered and said unto them, Give ye them to eat. And they say unto him, Shall we go and buy two hundred pennyworth of bread, and give them to eat? He saith unto them, How many loaves have ye? go and see. And when they knew, they say, Five, and two fishes. And he commanded them to make all sit down by companies upon the green grass. And they sat down in ranks, by hundreds, and by fifties. And when he had taken the five loaves and the two fishes, he looked up to heaven, and blessed, and brake the loaves, and gave them to his disciples to set before them; and the two fishes divided he among them all.*

And they did all eat, and were filled. And they took up twelve baskets full of the fragments, and of the fishes. And they that did eat of the loaves were about five thousand men. (Mark 6:34-44 – KJV)

This was a miracle. In his writings, the apostle Paul called it the working of miracles. Many miracles took place that day. Jesus only broke the bread and the fish twelve times as He gave a portion to each disciple. The bread and the fish multiplied each time the disciples gave some to the people— what an excellent example of these men doing the works of Jesus. Considering the sheer volume of what the disciples did, this could be regarded as even greater works. This raises another question. How does this illustrate preaching the gospel to the poor?

The gospel is the good news. We often only relate this to the most important good news. I am speaking of the good news of salvation. But in this passage, the need for good news is applied to the poor. It has been said many times that the best news for poor people is that they do not have to remain poor.

No doubt there were people in this crowd who could have purchased food for everyone present. While that would have been a nice gesture, how would this have been good news for them? No matter how much money a person may have, some unattainable things still exist. Money can't buy everything. In this respect, we are all poor. We must have God's help to do many things. For those who do not know God, this creates a type of poverty. Only the power of God and only the anointing of the Holy Spirit could do what happened that day.

It was so obvious that all of the Gospel writers felt compelled to tell the story.

The good news to the poor is that we are never without the resources to accomplish the task at hand as long as we have the anointing. I speak of the anointing only available because the Spirit of the Lord is upon us.

Some would only look at the miracle of these five thousand men plus the women and children being fed as something which met a physical need. It was much more than that. Others would look at the story and wonder where the preaching is. As I said earlier, actual preaching provokes action. The preaching is not just in words spoken. It is in the results. What lingers in the mind after the sermon is finished? What thoughts has the message provoked? Does it arouse further inquiry? Does the preaching make you want to do something?

Very little is said about the end of the story. *And they did all eat, and were filled. And they took up twelve baskets full of the fragments, and of the fishes.* Poor people rarely get to eat until they are filled. Even rarer is for there to be anything left over. I am presenting the challenge for our sermons to be shown, and I don't necessarily mean like this one. The illustration should come in the changes we see in the lives of those to whom we preach. There are many forms of poverty, but none the Gospel can't reach.

Another example of preaching the gospel to the poor is the story of the great catch of fish. This is also an illustration of the working of miracles, the word of knowledge, and the word of wisdom.

And it came to pass, that, as the people pressed upon him to hear the word of God, he stood by the lake of Gennesaret, And saw two ships standing by the lake: but the fishermen were gone out of them, and were washing their nets. And he entered into one of the ships, which was Simon's, and prayed him that he would thrust out a little from the land. And he sat down, and taught the people out of the ship. Now when he had left speaking, he said unto Simon, Launch out into the deep, and let down your nets for a draught. And Simon answering said unto him, Master, we have toiled all the night, and have taken nothing: nevertheless at thy word I will let down the net. And when they had this done, they enclosed a great multitude of fishes: and their net brake. And they beckoned unto their partners, which were in the other ship, that they should come and help them. And they came, and filled both the ships, so that they began to sink. When Simon Peter saw it, he fell down at Jesus' knees, saying, Depart from me; for I am a sinful man, O Lord. For he was astonished, and all that were with him, at the draught of the fishes which they had taken: And so was also James, and John, the sons of Zebedee, which were partners with Simon. And Jesus said unto Simon, Fear not; from henceforth thou shalt catch men. And when they had brought their ships to land, they forsook all, and followed him. (Luke 5:1-11 – KJV)

These fishermen may not have been people we would classify as poor. However, to have fished all night and caught nothing is a good indication that they were not feeling prosperous. Once again, I have taken the liberty to define what it means to be poor or rich in the context of the gifts of the Spirit. Consider what this revelation did for these men.

They learned from this experience that it was possible to know where to find a boatload of fish ahead of time. It seems too practical for religious-minded folks, but this is the way the gifts of the Spirit work.

They supernaturally solve natural problems that can't be solved any other way.

In both stories, Jesus wanted all these people to think like Paul when he wrote the following statement.

> *But my God shall supply all your need according to his riches in glory by Christ Jesus. (Philippians 4:19 – KJV)*

If we are going to do the works Jesus did and even greater works, we must learn to preach as Jesus preached. Our audiences should be preaching our messages by the results the anointing produces in their lives. After feeding the 5,000, those disciples may have gone away and bragged about the great meal they fed the people that evening. The men in the boat may have bragged about how many fish they caught. If they did, they missed the whole purpose of these miracles. Jesus wanted them to get a revelation that these were things they could do just as He had done.

There are millions of broken-hearted people in our world. The members of our family and our close friends have experienced broken hearts. Death is no respecter of persons. How did Jesus deal with this one? The story of Lazarus comes to my mind. In this story, we find examples of the working of miracles, the gifts of healing, the gift of faith, and the word of wisdom.

> *Now Jesus had not yet come into the town, but was in the place where Martha met Him. Then the Jews who were with her in the house, and comforting her, when they saw that Mary rose up quickly and went out, followed her, saying, "She is going to the tomb to weep there." Then, when Mary came where Jesus was, and saw Him, she fell down at His feet, saying to Him, "Lord, if You had been here, my brother would not have died." Therefore, when Jesus saw her weeping, and the Jews who came with her weeping, He groaned in the spirit and was troubled. And He said, "Where have you laid him?" They said to Him, "Lord, come and see." Jesus wept. Then the Jews said, "See how He loved him!" And some of them said, "Could not this Man, who opened the eyes of the blind, also have kept this man from dying?" Then Jesus, again groaning in Himself, came to the tomb. It was a cave, and a stone lay against it. Jesus said, "Take away the stone." Martha, the sister of him who was dead, said to Him, "Lord, by this time there is a stench, for he has been dead four days." Jesus said to her, "Did I not say to you that if you would believe you would see the glory of God?" Then they took away the stone from the place where the dead man was lying. And Jesus lifted up His eyes and said, "Father, I thank You that You have heard Me. And I know that You always hear Me, but because of the people who are standing by I said this, that they may believe that You sent Me." Now when He had said these things, He cried with a loud voice, "Lazarus, come forth!" And he*

who had died came out bound hand and foot with grave-clothes, and his face was wrapped with a cloth. Jesus said to them, "Loose him, and let him go."
(John 11:30-44 – NKJV)

It may not always be the will of God to raise a person from the dead. However, I believe this should happen far more often than we have seen. You can imagine what this would do for broken hearts. This requires a miracle. The person newly raised from the dead must also be cured of what caused them to die. Other gifts of the Spirit are no doubt involved. There is much to think about and meditate on in this story. We know of others Jesus raised from the dead. Without a doubt, He raised many we do not know about.

From the various references in the Bible, we can assume that Jesus spent considerable time casting out devils. He was bringing deliverance to the captives. This type of ministry requires the operation of more than one gift of the Spirit. There appears to be no question about the demonic activity in the following story. However, some would conclude that the man was insane. Did his mind need healing? Or were there demons to be cast out? Discerning of spirits is the gift that is required. Calmly approaching a person in this condition also involves the gift of faith.

Then they sailed to the country of the Gadarenes, which is opposite Galilee. And when He stepped out on the land, there met Him a certain man from the city who had demons for a long time. And he wore no clothes, nor did he live in a house but in the tombs. When he saw Jesus, he cried out, fell down before Him, and with a loud voice said, "What have I to do with You, Jesus, Son of the Most High God? I beg You, do not torment me!" For He had commanded the unclean spirit to come out of the man. For it had often seized him, and he was kept under guard, bound with chains and shackles; and he broke the bonds and was driven by the demon into the wilderness. Jesus asked him, saying, "What is your name?" And he said, "Legion," because many demons had entered him. And they begged Him that He would not command them to go out into the abyss. Now a herd of many swine was feeding there on the mountain. So they begged Him that He would permit them to enter them. And He permitted them. Then the demons went out of the man and entered the swine, and the herd ran violently down the steep place into the lake and drowned. When those who fed them saw what had happened, they fled and told it in the city and in the country. Then they went out to see what had happened, and came to Jesus, and found the man from whom the demons had departed, sitting at the feet of Jesus, clothed and in his right mind. And they were afraid. They also who had seen it told them by what means he who had been demon-possessed was healed. Then the whole multitude of the surrounding region of the Gadarenes asked Him to depart from them, for they were seized with great fear. And He got into the boat and returned. (Luke 8:26-37 – NKJV)

Many things stand out in this story. You will observe that Jesus spoke to the demonic spirits. Too often, we do not address the real problem when we encounter those held captive. For some reason, I do not understand there is an inclination to search for a source of the problem that does not include demons. Until we address the issue in people like this, our preaching does nothing. Casting out demons is more necessary than ever. They seem to be flourishing in their activity as the church is more concerned about other things.

I love the part about the request to go into the pigs. Animals can be possessed by demons. But the animals don't put up with it like people do. These animals could only tolerate this level of evil for a few minutes before they ran over the cliff. Now here is a remarkable part of this story.

The people in the region of the Gadarenes asked Jesus to leave, and He departed. **These people were more afraid of the power of the Holy Spirit than they were of a man possessed by demons.** Believe it or not, the same thing is true today. Much of the pressure being applied to obtain acceptance in society for the most perverse activity we can imagine is driven by this same fear. As strange as it may seem, some people are much more comfortable living with evil than living with the thought of being set free.

We should learn a lesson from Jesus. Instead of wasting time with those who do not want what we offer, we should turn to those who desire to be set free.

Chapter 15
It Takes a Revelation

Jesus never wasted words. Every time Jesus spoke, two things were evident. He was preaching or teaching the Word of God. And whatever the people needed to hear and receive was always available. In every audience where people came to hear Jesus speak, at least some people came to hear Jesus expecting something good to happen in their lives and those who expected good things received them.

His audiences always seemed to have included those who were poor, broken-hearted, or in need of deliverance. Many blind people came to hear Him and receive their sight. Those who were bruised because of dysfunctional families and broken relationships were drawn to Him. Despite it all, they wanted to hear Jesus preach about the acceptable year of the Lord.

The crowds never got enough. They wanted Jesus to keep teaching. Keep preaching. The good news He came to give drew them like a giant magnet. When He stopped and tried to go away to rest, the crowds followed Him. Something much more than mere words was being shared.

We call it a revelation.

The word **revelation** has been defined as 1) the act or process of disclosing something previously secret or obscure, especially something true, 2) a fact disclosed or revealed, especially in a dramatic or surprising way, 3) (Ecclesiastical Terms) Christianity, a.) God's disclosure of his own nature and his purpose for mankind, especially through the words of human intermediaries, b.) something in which such a divine disclosure is contained, such as the Bible.[34] This definition is repeated with a fourth heading labeled (Bible) Christianity.

For years I wrestled with these definitions and was sure there must be a better way to express what happens when the Word of God is taught or preached and is accompanied by the anointing. The profound impact seemed to indicate more than this definition expressed. To complicate matters further, I noticed this was very much an individual experience. While listening to the same message, one person would be deeply affected, and another nearby seemed uninterested. So, I have drawn my own conclusions about the term revelation.

I consider revelation to be an act inspired by the Holy Spirit. It never happens without Him. It is indeed personal. Thus, I express my definition of the word **revelation** in the following way. Keep in mind this comes from my experience and not from a Biblical language source.

Revelation is a truth
I did not know previously
and would never have known
without the help of the Holy Spirit.

You may know truth that I do not know and vice versa. The work of the Holy Spirit in this endeavor is unique and thrilling to observe. I have seen many lives change as revelation came to their hearts. Perhaps it will help if I state this in the following way.

Poor people will stay poor until they receive a revelation that they do not have to remain poor.

Brokenhearted people will stay brokenhearted until they receive a revelation that they do not have to remain brokenhearted.

Captives will stay bound and need deliverance until they receive a revelation that they can be free.

Blind people, and for that matter, every sick or diseased person, will stay sick or diseased until they receive a revelation that they can be well.

Those who are bruised will remain bruised until they receive a revelation that they can be healed.

Here is a story from the Bible that illustrates several things I have just said.

> *And one of the multitude answered and said, Master, I have brought unto thee my son, which hath a dumb spirit; And wheresoever he taketh him, he teareth him: and he foameth, and gnasheth with his teeth, and pineth away: and I spake to thy disciples that they should cast him out; and they could not. He answereth him, and saith, O faithless generation, how long shall I be with you? how long shall I suffer you? bring him unto me. And they*

brought him unto him: and when he saw him, straightway the spirit tare him; and he fell on the ground, and wallowed foaming. And he asked his father, How long is it ago since this came unto him? And he said, Of a child. And ofttimes it hath cast him into the fire, and into the waters, to destroy him: but if thou canst do anything, have compassion on us, and help us. Jesus said unto him, If thou canst believe, all things are possible to him that believeth. And straightway the father of the child cried out, and said with tears, Lord, I believe; help thou mine unbelief. When Jesus saw that the people came running together, he rebuked the foul spirit, saying unto him, Thou dumb and deaf spirit, I charge thee, come out of him, and enter no more into him. And the spirit cried, and rent him sore, and came out of him: and he was as one dead; insomuch that many said, He is dead. But Jesus took him by the hand, and lifted him up; and he arose. (Mark 9:17-27 – KJV)

This young man had suffered from this demonic possession since childhood. We can only imagine the emotional trauma and bruising this caused him and his family. The people in this story fit into several categories. I am sure they were brokenhearted over what was happening to their son. The boy needed deliverance and healing. The path to their ultimate victory was found in the revelation that came to this father.

The father, distraught over the disciples' failure in their attempt to cast out the demon, made an unusual request. These are his words to Jesus. *If thou canst do anything, have compassion on us, and help us.* This father was not sure Jesus would be successful. I have always wondered about that.

When Jesus responded to the man, a great revelation came to him. The disciples already knew the truth this man had discovered. What is of greater interest to me is the revelation I received one day as I read these verses. I suddenly realized that the punctuation is incorrect. I was struggling with the notion that this man might not be able to believe. This is the way it reads in the old *King James Bible.*

> *Jesus said unto him, If thou canst believe, all things are possible to him that believeth. (Mark 9:23 – KJV)*

This rendering implies that the problem was the inability of the man to believe. It has been taught in this way many times. If you can only believe, all things are possible. I do not think this is what Jesus said. Believing is always possible. It is a choice. The response from Jesus was both forceful and emphatic.

When the father said to Jesus, *If thou canst do anything,* I believe Jesus stopped him and shouted back at him – **If thou canst – what do you mean if I can?** Jesus was appalled at the audacity of this man, even in his moment of desperation to question the ability of the Lord Jesus to do anything about this demon. Jesus had won this battle centuries before. But this man did not know that. He did not have a revelation of the power and authority that belonged to Jesus.

Jesus said one word that changed everything – believe! Then Jesus followed this with an explanation which often happens when there is a revelation.

Those words were simple and powerful. *All things are possible to him that believeth.*

I preached this message one Sunday morning at the church where I was pastor. A lady in the audience approached my wife and asked her to give me this message. She told my wife she had heard another minister explain the story in the same way more than forty years before that time. The lady said she had asked the Lord to reveal this to another minister so she could hear it again. There was no recording of the first person she heard say these things. It was my privilege to be the answer to her prayer. I received the revelation and shared it.

On that day, standing in front of Jesus, this father received a revelation of what God could do. He discovered the authority Jesus had over the devil. His son was set free. The disciples did not yet have a revelation of the power they had been given. Thankfully they did receive this revelation later and acted on it many times.

For some time after that Sunday, when I taught this message, I wondered if I had been correct. I was excited to hear what this lady had told my wife. I knew the lady and had great respect for her. I was greatly encouraged years later when I read the following in the *Amplified Bible.*

> *And [Jesus] asked his father, How long has he had this? And he answered, From the time he was a little boy. And it has often thrown him both into fire and into water, intending to kill him. But if You can do anything, do have pity on us and help us. And Jesus said, [You say to Me], If You can do anything? [Why,] all things can be (are possible) to him who believes! At once the father of*

the boy gave [an eager, piercing, inarticulate] cry with tears, and he said, Lord, I believe! [Constantly] help my weakness of faith! (Mark 9:21-24 – AMPC)

What may at first seem to be only a word of correction that Jesus gave to this father is actually much more. Jesus exhorted the man to believe. The revelation that Jesus could help the boy was edifying and comforting. As a result, this fits the definition of a prophecy that the apostle Paul gave in the following verse.

He that prophesieth speaketh unto men to edification, and exhortation, and comfort. (1 Corinthians 14:3 – KJV)

I love the stories in the Gospels of the blind receiving their sight. It must be a terrible thing to be blind. I don't know if it would be worse never to see or have your vision and lose it. Both are very traumatic. But the power of the Holy Ghost is the answer to both situations. Let's look at the story of Bartimaeus. It is one of my favorites.

And they came to Jericho: and as he went out of Jericho with his disciples and a great number of people, blind Bartimaeus, the son of Timaeus, sat by the highway side begging. And when he heard that it was Jesus of Nazareth, he began to cry out, and say, Jesus, thou son of David, have mercy on me. And many charged him that he should hold his peace: but he cried the more a great deal, Thou son of David, have mercy on me. And Jesus stood still, and commanded him to be called. And they call the blind man, saying unto him, Be of good comfort, rise; he calleth thee. And he, casting away his garment, rose, and came to Jesus. And Jesus answered and said

unto him, What wilt thou that I should do unto thee?
The blind man said unto him, Lord, that I might receive
my sight. And Jesus said unto him, Go thy way; thy faith
hath made thee whole. And immediately he received his
sight, and followed Jesus in the way.
(Mark 10:46-52 – KJV)

This story has deep meaning to me for two reasons. The first was the difference in the response of this blind man when Jesus spoke to Him as compared to the father of the boy who had a demon. The blind man did not question that Jesus could heal him. He knew Jesus had the ability. The revelation the blind man needed was concerning the willingness of Jesus to heal him. To state this succinctly, this was a poor blind beggar. The disciples had treated him like all the other people did. They demanded that he be quiet and not bother the Master. Would Jesus care enough about him to open his blind eyes?

The glorious answer is an absolute yes!

This story means so much to me because one of the first miracles I saw was when a girl born blind received her sight. She was in the audience when I preached one night in South Africa. The Holy Spirit gave me a word of knowledge and a word of wisdom for her. I did not know this young lady. But the Holy Ghost showed me where she sat in that crowd of about six thousand people.

I pointed in her direction, and said, "A lady is sitting right back there who is blind. If you stand to your feet, you will receive your sight." She jumped to her feet and screamed, "I can see!" She ran up the aisle, telling everybody she passed as she made her way to the front of the building that she could now see. This is an experience I will never forget. This was not my imagination. People in the crowd confirmed that this girl had been born completely blind. The influence of this miracle was tremendous. It profoundly impacted a large denomination that did not believe in divine healing. They, too, began to minister to the sick and saw great results.

I choose to take those words Jesus spoke in the synagogue very personally. The Spirit of the Lord is upon me, because He has anointed me.

Now we come to the final part of this passage. Jesus said He was anointed to *preach the acceptable year of the Lord*. What is this all about? How do you preach this, and what does it mean?

Many Biblical translations state that this refers to a particular time of God's favor. Or, as some have said, this is a time when humanity has favor with God. These are exciting explanations of the year of the Lord. For the Jews on earth, simultaneously as Jesus, this would have been considered a very prophetic message. This is commonly called a word of wisdom because it refers to the future. Any comments or future predictions are often called words of wisdom, even if they meet none of the other aspects of this gift. For many years the Jewish people had not seen God's favor.

They had lived in bondage to one empire after another. This was true not only for the contemporaries of Jesus but also for their parents and grandparents.

While the notion of *the acceptable year of the Lord* holds little meaning for us, it had significant meaning for the Jews. I feel sure they were all familiar with what is known as the Year of Jubilee. This was structured into their culture as an event every fifty years. It was an extraordinary time, as described in the book of Leviticus.

> *The LORD said to Moses at Mount Sinai, "Speak to the Israelites and say to them: 'When you enter the land I am going to give you, the land itself must observe a sabbath to the LORD. For six years sow your fields, and for six years prune your vineyards and gather their crops. But in the seventh year the land is to have a year of sabbath rest, a sabbath to the LORD. Do not sow your fields or prune your vineyards. "'Count off seven sabbath years—seven times seven years—so that the seven sabbath years amount to a period of forty-nine years. Then have the trumpet sounded everywhere on the tenth day of the seventh month; on the Day of Atonement sound the trumpet throughout your land. Consecrate the fiftieth year and proclaim liberty throughout the land to all its inhabitants. It shall be a jubilee for you; each of you is to return to your family property and to your own clan. The fiftieth year shall be a jubilee for you; do not sow and do not reap what grows of itself or harvest the untended vines. For it is a jubilee and is to be holy for you; eat only what is taken directly from the fields. "'In this Year of Jubilee, everyone is to return to their own property. (Leviticus 25:1-4, 8-13 – NIV)*

Most, if not all, of the people in the synagogue, knew all these details. More importantly, since they had never experienced this marvelous provision and knew they probably never would, they must have wondered why Jesus read about this. What could be going through His mind? Why preach about something they had never seen?

Go back to the opinions about the acceptable year of the Lord I stated previously. I said it was a time of favor. The word grace is often defined as unmerited favor. However, *Strong's Concordance* presents a better understanding of the Greek word **charis**. I am particularly fond of the following statement.

(Grace is) goodwill, loving-kindness, favor. (It speaks) of the merciful kindness by which God, exerting his holy influence upon souls, turns them to Christ, keeps, strengthens, increases them in Christian faith, knowledge, affection, and kindles them to the exercise of the Christian virtues.[35]

The apostle Paul penned these beautiful words to the Christians at Ephesus.

> *Blessed be the God and Father of our Lord Jesus Christ, who hath blessed us with all spiritual blessings in heavenly places in Christ: According as he hath chosen us in him before the foundation of the world, that we should be holy and without blame before him in love: Having predestinated us unto the adoption of children by Jesus Christ to himself, according to the good pleasure of his will, To the praise of the glory of his grace, wherein he hath made us accepted in the beloved.*
> *(Ephesians 1:3-6 – KJV)*

We no longer must wait for fifty years to go by to celebrate our place in God. As born-again believers, we have been accepted in the beloved. We have His love, His grace, and His blessing. We are never without it. Think of this as one very long year. God is always wanting to bless us, and yet many people don't know it.

It is the year of the Lord.
It is not the year of man, either Jew or Gentile.

This is God's year!

Our time on earth is called the time of grace. It is a time of great favor. So far, it has lasted over two thousand years. It will continue until the return of the Lord Jesus.

The anointing on Jesus presided over the beginning of this year of acceptance because of His death, burial, and resurrection. Jesus preached it before it happened. Our great joy is to proclaim this year of blessing and favor until He returns.

In the stories I have shared, I have attempted to give examples of each of the seven gifts of the Spirit, which were prolific in the ministry of Jesus.

Chapter 16
Excitement in the Synagogue

When Jesus had finished reading the passage from Isaiah chapter 61, He sat down and looked at the crowd of people in the synagogue. Every eye was on Him. The atmosphere was electrified with anticipation. From the group's reaction, it was already clear Jesus was making a very personal application of these tremendous words of prophecy. He believed this prophecy was about Him. Many of these people had heard the stories of what had happened in His meetings as He taught and healed the sick. What would Jesus say and do next? I doubt any of them expected to hear these words.

This day is this scripture fulfilled in your ears.
(Luke 4:21 – KJV)

What could this mean? Sure, they heard what Jesus read. But what did He mean by such a strange statement? They were about to find out, and some would be very happy. But as it always seemed to be when Jesus spoke, some of the crowd was about to become very angry. The truth seems to have that effect on some people. But what does this strange statement mean?

If Jesus had only said: This day is this scripture fulfilled, this statement would be easy to understand. We would probably skip over this sentence and move on to the rest of the story. But indeed, something important is intended by these words. The Greek word translated **fulfilled** in the text means to **ratify** or accomplish.[36] This definitely merits further investigation. We know from reading many of the things Jesus said, He constantly desired for much more to happen than for the people to only hear what He had to say. While hearing is the first step, it is not the final step. Jesus expected the people to do something with what they had heard.

Jesus wanted it to be clear this prophecy was about Him. These are the things He came to earth to do. Jesus desired to make sure that these people knew what He had just read about was available to them. These were His friends. This was His hometown. Without a doubt, there were people in the audience who needed healing. There may have been people who were brokenhearted. To set these people free of things holding some of them captive would have been a great thing. But none of these things happened. Why?

Because these scriptures were only fulfilled in their ears.

I find the use of the Greek word for **ratify** to be informative. When a document is ratified, it commonly means it is approved and becomes legally binding on those who ratified it. If the document applies to a large group of people, such as a law that a state government passes, then it applies to everyone in that state. It is impossible to know how much of this the people in the synagogue understood. However, from their reaction, they understood it very well. In one sense, it seemed to them that Jesus was insisting they believe these things about Him. **He was!**

If they had only believed what He said, He was ready and able to prove He could do the things He had claimed He could do. Instead, they allowed these words to stop in their ears and never reach their heart.

Don't you wonder why they did not give Jesus a chance to prove what He said? If they had done so, and it turned out to be accurate, what had they lost? Or, on the other hand, what would they have gained? This could have been a life-changing moment. I am astounded at their unbelief.

To enhance our understanding of the phrase regarding the ears, it is helpful to address the first part of the verse I just quoted. The entire statement is as follows.

And he began to say unto them; This day is this scripture fulfilled in your ears. (Luke 4:21 – KJV)

The typical reader tends to change those first few words in their mind as they read. What they see is, "and Jesus said" or "and Jesus added." Drawing this conclusion completely changes the meaning of the verse. Jesus had many more things He wanted to share with these people.

The very words, *He began to say* convey that Jesus never finished what He wanted to say. He realized they were not accepting that this prophecy was about Him. Knowing His words would only fall on spiritually deaf ears, Jesus chose not to go any further with an explanation of the prophecy from Isaiah. I wish they had not stopped Him. We might have a tremendous explanation of these verses if He had been allowed to continue.

Revelation always requires
a continuous flow of embrace.

Every genuine revelation comes in stages or steps. When we grasp one level of revelation, another usually follows. Depending on the need and the subject, the revelation will grow as we believe what God shares with us. This is the reason the Bible is so rich in meaning. It is a continuous unfolding of the revelation of God and His relationship with the man He created.

We begin with God, and with Him, there is no end.

I am surprised at the translation of this verse in some of the well-respected Bible translations, such as the *Holman Christian Standard Bible.*

> *He began by saying to them, "Today as you listen, this Scripture has been fulfilled." (Luke 4:21 – HCSB)*

This translation leaves the impression Jesus had completed the prophecy given by Isaiah. He had only begun to do the things Isaiah prophesied. At this point, Jesus had healed a few sick people. But, as far as we know, He had not raised anyone from the dead. As large as His crowds may have been, He had not fed thousands of people or walked on water and calmed the raging seas.

My reaction to this translation and others similar is that none of the six things Jesus had come to do took place in the synagogue as they listened. He only said He was anointed to do these things. This translation and others imply miraculous things were happening in the synagogue. There is no indication of such activity. He did not do any of them in front of them. Here is another very poor translation example of this statement.

> He began to say to them, "Today this Scripture has been fulfilled, as you've heard it read aloud."
> (Luke 4:21 – ISV)

As He read these Scriptures aloud, the only thing that happened was that they heard Him reading. What were these translators missing? They failed to grasp the meaning of these words. Therefore, they also missed the reason for the reaction of the people in His hometown who knew Jesus from a very early age. If we only consider these words as they have often been translated, it is impossible to understand why some people were so offended.

Good Biblical translation does not occur unless the entire context of Scripture is considered. Sadly, many linguistic experts in the Greek and Hebrew languages are not equally adept in Theology. They often do not take the Bible as factually correct. It is common for these brilliant people to have a particular bias regarding the purpose of the Bible. It was written not as a history book but that we might believe in all that Jesus came to say and do.

The Bible is a living document.

The message of the Bible is as relevant today as it was the day it was written. The various authors may not have known people other than those they addressed themselves who would fully embrace their words. But we do. When I read the Bible, I treat these statements as though they were written specifically for me. I believe every person should have the same attitude. The Bible is the book I choose to live by. There is no more significant source of direction for life. So, when I read what Jesus said, my attitude about the Bible greatly influences my understanding.

It will be helpful to explain what it means for something to be fulfilled in your ears. Sometime after this event in the synagogue, Jesus gave insight into this matter of the Scripture being fulfilled in our ears. When something is fulfilled, we consider it to be complete. The desired or anticipated results have come to fruition.

Jesus pointed out the danger of assuming that hearing alone was sufficient. Several verses address this issue. One statement often connected to the teaching of Jesus is expressed in the gospel of Matthew.

> *Other seeds fell on good soil and produced grain, some a hundredfold, some sixty, some thirty. He who has ears, let him hear." (Matthew 13:8-9 – ESV)*

Jesus was using a parable in His teaching. He broke the topic into four sections to enhance the parable's meaning, each represented by a different soil type. The verse above is the words Jesus spoke as He ended the parable. He was sure the disciples did not understand the meaning of the parable and sure enough, they requested an explanation.

Once the parable's purpose is understood, we can grasp the meaning of the words: *He who has ears to hear, let him hear.*

The parable's purpose was to keep the people who did not believe in Jesus from understanding His teaching. If they understood, they would be held accountable for not doing what Jesus said. Jesus did not want this to happen.

Those who do not want to understand do not have ears to hear. Those who do not think it is important to understand spiritual truths do not have ears to hear. Those who are unwilling to take the time to understand what God has said do not have ears to hear.

All of those in the crowd heard with their natural ears. They understood the words, but they did not have ears to hear. They did not go to the synagogue to learn. The entire experience was only about the fact that they went to the synagogue. They expected nothing good or bad to happen. They were content with what their natural ears could hear. But having natural ears with perfect natural hearing is not sufficient—our inner man must listen also.

We are spirit beings. We only live in this body as long as we are residents of this earth. Your spirit can hear. Most of the time God speaks to your spirit, not to your mind. When a person speaks of being led by the spirit, he talks about his spirit hearing what the Holy Ghost is saying.

These are strong, valid spiritual principles. Yet, many people do not know them and certainly do not understand them. The result is depicted in what happened in the synagogue. The people heard what Jesus said with their natural ears. But their spiritual understanding was non-existent.

It was as though they heard nothing of benefit.

If the words Jesus had just read had been fulfilled as the people listened, miracles would have happened. I am sure you noticed the translation of the scripture in Luke found in the *Holman Christian Standard Bible*, and the *International Standard Version* does not include the reference to the ears of the people. The translators of these versions of the Bible concluded that the only important thing to be fulfilled that day was identifying who the subject of Isaiah's prophecy was.

This was not the same opinion Jesus had. He continued to make this very clear.

Jesus was not just speaking to the crowd in the synagogue.

I think Luke knew this. Instinctively, or if you prefer, by the inspiration of the Holy Ghost, Luke knew Jesus was saying something for people in the ages to come.

Yes, those words apply to what would follow that day in the synagogue. I am saying they were much more potent than we might assume. This was a transitional statement. Verse 21 points to the words Jesus was about to speak. It also reflects on the words Jesus had already said.

In a more ordinary manner of speaking, Jesus lit a fire in the synagogue. **Jesus started something that, after two thousand years, has not stopped. The blaze burns brighter today than it ever has. The anointing is more robust than it has ever been.** The Spirit of the Lord is resting on more people today than ever. Jesus knew He was starting a move of the Spirit on this planet that would never stop. Yes, it rises and falls in momentum. But it will never stop.

We will look carefully at the rest of what Jesus said and the reaction His words caused. I only want you to realize that what happened in the synagogue was the beginning of something great. It was not the end.

The strange statement found in this same verse is the best indicator I have to prove my conclusion is correct. Once you understand the meaning, the rest becomes obvious.

For many of these people, being in the synagogue and hearing Jesus read these words and imply they were talking about Him was the only thing that happened. His words got no further than their natural hearing. Thus, they were fulfilled in their ears. There would be no further benefit. As Jesus continued to speak, things got much worse. To help us understand the events which followed, we should consider the following story.

> *Jesus left there and went to his hometown, accompanied by his disciples. When the Sabbath came, he began to teach in the synagogue, and many who heard him were amazed. "Where did this man get these things?" they asked. "What's this wisdom that has been given him? What are these remarkable miracles he is performing? Isn't this the carpenter? Isn't this Mary's son and the brother of James, Joseph, Judas and Simon? Aren't his sisters here with us?" And they took offense at him. Jesus said to them, "A prophet is not without honor except in his own town, among his relatives and in his own home."*
> *He could not do any miracles there, except lay his hands on a few sick people and heal them.*
> *(Mark 6:1-5 – NIV)*

I am inclined to believe that this may be the same event as the one recorded in the gospel of Luke. Some are bothered by the apparent difference in the timing of these two Biblical records. It has amused me to consider how much the opinion of scholars is forced upon the Scripture writers. Just because we would like to have these events in an exact chronological order does not impact what was written. It seems to me incredibly flawed to consider these differences to be contradictions. These men were endeavoring to record their personal experiences as they remembered them. They cannot be regarded as journalists who recorded every move Jesus made and every word He said. We do not hold journalists to this extreme level in our day. They show different pictures from different vantage points as they tell their stories. We do not expect a precise word-for-word account of their reports.

Why, then, is the Bible often treated differently unless it is to create doubt?

Jesus knew what was possible if the people would only listen and believe. He also knew what would happen if they did not. We have expressed in Mark's account a clear explanation of why we do not see more miracles.

> *He could not do any miracles there, except lay his hands on a few sick people and heal them. He was amazed at their lack of faith. (Mark 6:5-6 – NIV)*

To say Jesus could not do any miracles in His hometown needs an explanation. Mark provides it in the next verse. I am providing this in the *New King James Version* because I believe it is much more precise than the *New International Version*.

214

Now He could do no mighty work there, except that He laid His hands on a few sick people and healed them. And He marveled because of their unbelief. Then He went about the villages in a circuit, teaching. (Mark 6:5-6 – NKJV)

Unbelief was the problem. Some have pointed to the fact that Jesus was in the presence of people who had known Him since He was born as the reason for His inability to perform miracles. The correct way to view this is to consider this familiarity as the cause of the unbelief. Being personally acquainted with a person whom God uses extensively is not the problem. It is how we allow this personal acquaintance to impact our ability to believe.

It is a shocking thought, but Jesus was utterly stopped from doing what He had gone to His hometown to do. Considering what Jesus had done in other places, He went there to heal every sick person in His hometown. He would have cast out every demon and cleansed every leper. He only healed a few sick people.

This part of the story reveals another vital piece of information. When Jesus could not do the miracles and could not heal every sick person, He realized the real problem. He also knew the answer to the problem. The people needed to be taught. They did not know all they needed to know. The right kind of knowledge from the right source can produce faith. It is faith that receives from God. The apostle Paul stated it very well.

So then faith comes by hearing, and hearing by the word of God. (Romans 10:17 – NKJV)

Once again, we are addressing the subject of hearing. Hearing the Word of God is only the first step. Faith becomes available at this point. However, it is so often true that nothing happens due to this hearing. Great things from the Word of God may have been shared. This was certainly true when Jesus read the scriptures in the synagogue. Understanding what has been read is very important in the development of faith.

Yet, many things in the Bible are so simple that they do not require much explanation. For example, how much more needs to be said than that Jesus is present to heal blind eyes and broken hearts? There is another missing element.

It is action. One must respond to God's Word with actions that indicate they believe what they have heard. Challenging the source of what is being said is not the correct reaction. When the crowd in the synagogue made it clear they only saw Jesus as the boy who grew up in their town and not the one Isaiah spoke about, they were not demonstrating the right action. They were making it obvious they did not believe Jesus could do all that had been prophesied.

This crowd made a decision not to believe. The words doubt and unbelief are often used together as though they are two words expressing the same thing. My observation has taught me that this is not the case. **Doubt** is an excellent word to use for the actions of a **person who has not yet made up their mind to believe**. On the other hand, **unbelief** is a perfect word to describe the actions, comments, and attitudes of **those who have decided not to believe**.

Unbelief is very dangerous.

Now we must turn our attention to the rest of the events in the synagogue. To say the least, the reaction of this group of people is shocking. I find it very hard to imagine a group of people could be this cruel.

> *So all bore witness to Him, and marveled at the gracious words which proceeded out of His mouth. And they said, "Is this not Joseph's son?" He said to them, "You will surely say this proverb to Me, 'Physician, heal yourself! Whatever we have heard done in Capernaum, do also here in Your country.' " Then He said, "Assuredly, I say to you, no prophet is accepted in his own country. But I tell you truly, many widows were in Israel in the days of Elijah, when the heaven was shut up three years and six months, and there was a great famine throughout all the land; but to none of them was Elijah sent except to Zarephath, in the region of Sidon, to a woman who was a widow. And many lepers were in Israel in the time of Elisha the prophet, and none of them was cleansed except Naaman the Syrian." So all those in the synagogue, when they heard these things, were filled with wrath, and rose up and thrust Him out of the city; and they led Him to the brow of the hill on which their city was built, that they might throw Him down over the cliff. Then passing through the midst of them, He went His way. (Luke 4:22-30 – NKJV)*

First, they thought His words were gracious. But immediately, some in the same group made it clear they did not believe this prophecy could be about Jesus. He was only the son of the local carpenter. It was as though Jesus could read their thoughts. When people are not thinking what they should be thinking, and you let them know that you know it, they are never happy.

Consider these words. *Whatever we have heard done in Capernaum, do also here in Your country.* They would have stated this challenge had He only waited. The challenge is not important. It is the meaning we must understand.

These people embraced no responsibility for the fulfillment of the prophecy. They saw no need to believe. It was completely up to Jesus to make it happen. This is a strange but common concept of how God does things. It is not always the same wording because we live in a different world, but people still make statements like this.

Why didn't God stop the tornado that killed those people and destroyed their homes? Why didn't God prevent that plane crash that killed two hundred people? Why didn't God destroy the disease that made so many people sick; some even died?

This is the same way of thinking Jesus encountered. The answer is the same today as it was the day Jesus said these words. We have a great deal of responsibility for what happens in our lives. This is true for every person, whether they are a Christian or an atheist.

As Jesus proceeded to point out the failure of the ancestors of this group of people, they became furious. There is a great lesson to be learned from the illustrations Jesus gave concerning personal responsibility. Each person is responsible for their own faith. Each one must do what is necessary to acquire faith and see that it grows strong. No one has the right or privilege to be an unbeliever. Yes, a person can choose to live in unbelief. But they will pay a huge price for doing so.

During the days of Elijah, many widows suffered greatly, and it was not Elijah's fault. During the days of Elisha, many lepers were in the land, and it was not Elisha's fault.

Jesus was making an explicit declaration. He told them He could solve their problems, but He was not going to take any responsibility or accept any blame for them continuing to have those problems if they rejected Him. Jesus was and is the Son of God. This has not changed. It may sound harsh, but it isn't.

After everything Jesus has done to make every promise in the Word of God a reality in our lives, it is not harsh, or mean for Him to expect something from us. All He has ever asked is that we believe what He has said. Act like we believe what He has said. Talk like we believe what He has said. We call it faith. Compared to the crucifixion, it isn't much to expect.

Those words make some people mad. I have a great deal of first-hand experience with that part of the story. These people became furious with Jesus. People are still doing that. At least in the United States and many other parts of the world, they can't do what these people did and get by with it.

They led Jesus to the brow of a hill and were going to push Him over the cliff and kill Him. I don't have words to express my reaction to this level of anger, hatred, and unbelief. They were unsuccessful. That is the good news. This was not the way Jesus was meant to die. Verse 30 is amazing. *Then passing through the midst of them, He went His way.*

Don't you know this was a shock? I wonder how long they looked for Him and asked each other where He went. If nothing else had convinced them that the Holy Ghost anointed Jesus, this should have. If nothing else convinced them the Spirit of the Lord was upon Jesus, this should have.

When the devil did not get what he wanted from Jesus in the wilderness temptation, he had the good sense to leave. These people were not functioning at that level. Jesus had to slip away from them. Religion and tradition and customs had a powerful hold on these people.

Jesus had taken them back to a time when great prophets they revered were on this earth. He had made it clear what was expected. It is essential for the Word of God to get beyond our ears and into our hearts. To receive anything from God, we must believe.

Being a good person is not enough. Being a good Jew is not enough. Being a good Christian is not enough. Being the best Christian anyone has ever known is not the way to be healed. Neither is it the way to have your financial needs met. It always has required hearing, believing, acting, and receiving what God has promised.

Now, perhaps it is easier to understand these words. *This day is this scripture fulfilled in your ears.*

Jesus set things in motion that day in the synagogue. These are things we can still benefit from today. It is up to us. The words can stop in our ears. Or we can allow the Holy Spirit to work in our hearts. The Holy Ghost has been sent to us for a particular purpose. John recorded these words of Jesus.

Howbeit when he, the Spirit of truth, is come, he will guide you into all truth: for he shall not speak of himself; but whatsoever he shall hear, that shall he speak: and he will shew you things to come. (John 16:13 – KJV)

Our Heavenly Father knew we were going to need help. We do not always take the things we hear and adequately use them. Often it is because we only listened to a little of the truth. It may or may not have been our fault. We are never without the help we need. The Holy Spirit is always with us, just as He was always with Jesus.

When Jesus walked away from His hometown, He was not running away from a problem. He knew He needed to teach those who would listen. And He did. Some would have never gone back to Nazareth. At least for a time, this would have been wise. We can't run from everything in life. At some time, we must learn a better way to deal with our battles. The Holy Spirit was there to help Jesus, and He is here to help you. What do you need the Holy Spirit to teach you? The Holy Spirit is more than ready to guide us into all truth.

My goal has been to show you that no matter what Jesus faced, the Holy Spirit was always there for Him. The Holy Spirit was always at work in His life. Jesus taught us that He was anointed. He has also taught us that we are anointed. It is the same anointing by the same Spirit.

It is now our right and privilege to live in the Spirit and walk in the Spirit, even as Jesus did in His life. Do we have more to learn? Yes. We always will.

Thank God for the Holy Ghost!

Notes

[1] works - "G2041 - ergon - Strong's Greek Lexicon (kjv)." Blue Letter Bible. Web. 3 May, 2023.
<https://www.blueletterbible.org/lexicon/g2041/kjv/tr/0-1/>.

[2] Written as a poem by Episcopal clergyman Phillips Brooks in 1867, two years after he visited Bethlehem. Now in Public Domain.

[3] The following information was taken from www.gotquestions.org. I do not vouch for the accuracy of this quote.

Three major options exist for interpreting this verse. First, it may be that Matthew is associating the word Nazarene with the Hebrew word netser ("branch or sprout"). The "Branch" was a common term for the Messiah, such as in Isaiah 11:1: "A shoot will come up from the stump of Jesse; from his roots a Branch will bear fruit." Hebrew was written with only consonants, and netser would have appeared as NZR—the same main consonants as Nazareth. In fact, in Aramaic, the common language of Jesus' day, the word for "Nazareth" and the Hebrew word for "branch" sounded very much alike. Matthew's point could be that Jesus was "sprouting up" from an obscure village in Galilee; Jesus was the Branch predicted by the prophets, and the name of the town He grew up in happens to sound just like the prophets' word for "branch."

A second option is that Matthew is citing a prophecy not found in the Old Testament but in another source. If so, Matthew referred to a prophecy known to his original audience yet unknown to us today. However, this is unlikely and an argument from silence.

A third option is that Matthew uses the word Nazarene in reference to a person who is "despised and rejected."

In the first century, Nazareth was a small town about 55 miles north of Jerusalem, and it had a negative reputation among the Jews.

Galilee was generally looked down upon by Judeans, and Nazareth of Galilee was especially despised (see John 1:46). If this was Matthew's emphasis, the prophecies Matthew had in mind could include Psalm 22:6-7 and Isaiah 53:3.

If Psalm 22:6–7 and Isaiah 53:3 are the prophecies that Matthew had in mind, then the meaning of "He shall be called a Nazarene" is something akin to "He shall be despised and mocked by His own people." Jesus not only identified with humanity by coming to our world; He also identified with the lowly of this world. His upbringing in an obscure and despised town served as an important part of His mission. Jesus identified Himself as "Jesus of Nazareth" during His encounter with Saul on the road to Damascus (Acts 22:7–8). After his conversion, Paul mentioned Jesus of Nazareth (Acts 26:9), and the term Nasara, meaning "Nazarene," is still used today by Muslims to identify a Christian.

[4] doctors - "G1320 - didaskalos - Strong's Greek Lexicon (kjv)." Blue Letter Bible. Web. 3 May, 2023.
<https://www.blueletterbible.org/lexicon/g1320/kjv/tr/0-1/>.

[5] Quora is an American social question-and-answer website based in Mountain View, California. It was founded on June 25, 2009, and made available to the public on June 21, 2010. Users can collaborate by editing questions and commenting on answers that have been submitted by other users. Wikipedia

[6] This information was taken from an article called "Doves as Pets" by Chewy Editorial and published on July 24, 2012.

[7] rush - "H6743 - ṣālēaḥ - Strong's Hebrew Lexicon (kjv)." Blue Letter Bible. Web. 4 May, 2023.
<https://www.blueletterbible.org/lexicon/h6743/kjv/wlc/0-1/>.

[8] The New Catholic Bible (Luke 3:23)

   a. Luke 3:23 gives a genealogy that is meant not as a historical document but as the assertion of a legal status. Jesus is linked to Joseph, even though it was known that the link was not one of blood; the reason for doing so is that at that time only men and not women had rights. The genealogy then moves back to David, without following the line of kings. From that point it continues again, not only as far as Abraham, but—and this is the chief novelty of the passage— as far as Adam, who comes from the hand of God. Luke's intention is to stress the point that Jesus belongs not only to the chosen people but to the entire human race, which he has come to save.

   Whereas Matthew specifically mentions three groups of 14 generations, Luke lists 77 names, according to a scheme of sevens. From the beginning of the human race until Jesus there are eleven series of seven (11 x 7). Jesus comes as Messiah in the eschatological stage of history (see 4 Esdras 14:11).

   b. Luke 3:23 It may be helpful to record another interpretation of the difference between this genealogy and that of Matthew: in virtue of the law of the levirate, Joseph (it is said) had two fathers, one biological (Jacob), the other legal (Heli); thus two different lists are used as far back as Shealtiel.

[9] drove - "G1544 - ekballō - Strong's Greek Lexicon (kjv)." Blue Letter Bible. Web. 4 May, 2023.
<https://www.blueletterbible.org/lexicon/g1544/kjv/tr/0-1/>.

[10] led - "G71 - agō - Strong's Greek Lexicon (kjv)." Blue Letter Bible. Web. 4 May, 2023.
<https://www.blueletterbible.org/lexicon/g71/kjv/tr/0-1/>.

[11] led - "G321 - anagō - Strong's Greek Lexicon (kjv)." Blue Letter Bible. Web. 4 May, 2023.
<https://www.blueletterbible.org/lexicon/g321/kjv/tr/0-1/>.

[12] temptation - "G3985 - peirazō - Strong's Greek Lexicon (kjv)." Blue Letter Bible. Web. 10 Feb, 2022. <https://www.blueletterbible.org/lexicon/g3985/kjv/tr/0-1/>.

[13] immediately - "G2112 - eutheōs - Strong's Greek Lexicon (kjv)." Blue Letter Bible. Web. 15 Feb, 2022. <https://www.blueletterbible.org/lexicon/g2112/kjv/tr/0-1/>.

[14] pleasures or lusts - "G2237 - hēdonē - Strong's Greek Lexicon (kjv)." Blue Letter Bible. Web. 15 Feb, 2022. <https://www.blueletterbible.org/lexicon/g2237/kjv/tr/0-1/>.

[15] strengthening - "G1765 - enischyō - Strong's Greek Lexicon (kjv)." Blue Letter Bible. Web. 15 Feb, 2022. <https://www.blueletterbible.org/lexicon/g1765/kjv/tr/0-1/>.

[16] "inspirit." American Heritage® Dictionary of the English Language, Fifth Edition. 2011. Houghton Mifflin Harcourt Publishing Company 15 Feb. 2022 https://www.thefreedictionary.com/inspirit

[17] "inspirit." Random House Kernerman Webster's College Dictionary. 2010. 2010 K Dictionaries Ltd. Copyright 2005, 1997, 1991 by Random House, Inc. 15 Feb. 2022 https://www.thefreedictionary.com/inspirit

[18] kingdoms - "G932 - basileia - Strong's Greek Lexicon (kjv)." Blue Letter Bible. Web. 16 Feb, 2022. <https://www.blueletterbible.org/lexicon/g932/kjv/tr/0-1/>.

[19] jurisdiction - "G1849 - exousia - Strong's Greek Lexicon (kjv)." Blue Letter Bible. Web. 3 May, 2022. https://www.blueletterbible.org/lexicon/g1849/kjv/tr/0-1/>.

[20] authority - "G1849 - exousia - Strong's Greek Lexicon (kjv)." Blue Letter Bible. Web. 15 Feb, 2022. <https://www.blueletterbible.org/lexicon/g1849/kjv/tr/0-1/>.

[21] jurisdiction - "G1849 - exousia - Strong's Greek Lexicon (kjv)." Blue Letter Bible. Web. 11 Apr, 2022. <https://www.blueletterbible.org/lexicon/g1849/kjv/tr/0-1/>. This word is only used one time to mean - jurisdiction – the devil's power had been relegated to him by men – think roman empire – the enemies of Israel.

[22] jurisdiction - American Heritage® Dictionary of the English Language, Fifth Edition. 2011. Houghton Mifflin Harcourt Publishing Company 16 Feb. 2022 https://www.thefreedictionary.com/jurisdiction

[23] jurisdiction - "G1849 - exousia - Strong's Greek Lexicon (kjv)." Blue Letter Bible. Web. 3 May, 2022. https://www.blueletterbible.org/lexicon/g1849/kjv/tr/0-1/>.

[24] power - "G1411 - dynamis - Strong's Greek Lexicon (kjv)." Blue Letter Bible. Web. 16 Feb, 2022. <https://www.blueletterbible.org/lexicon/g1411/kjv/tr/0-1/>.

[25] Ibid.

[26] world - "G3625 - oikoumenē - Strong's Greek Lexicon (kjv)." Blue Letter Bible. Web. 16 Feb, 2022. <https://www.blueletterbible.org/lexicon/g3625/kjv/tr/0-1/>.

[27] "Harmony of the Gospels - Study Resources - Study Resources." Blue Letter Bible. Web. 3 May, 2022. <https://www.blueletterbible.org/study/harmony/index.cfm>.

[28] shew - "G518 - apangellō - Strong's Greek Lexicon (kjv)." Blue Letter Bible. Web. 11 Apr, 2022. <https://www.blueletterbible.org/lexicon/g518/kjv/tr/0-1/>.

[29] anoint - "G5548 - chriō - Strong's Greek Lexicon (kjv)." Blue Letter Bible. Web. 11 Apr, 2022. <https://www.blueletterbible.org/lexicon/g5548/kjv/tr/0-1/>.

[30] endued - "G1746 - endyō - Strong's Greek Lexicon (kjv)." Blue Letter Bible. Web. 11 Apr, 2022. <https://www.blueletterbible.org/lexicon/g1746/kjv/tr/0-1/>.

[31] endue - American Heritage® Dictionary of the English Language, Fifth Edition. 2011. Houghton Mifflin Harcourt Publishing Company 11 Apr. 2022 https://www.thefreedictionary.com/endue

[32] Lester Sumrall, "The Gifts and Ministries of the Holy Spirit" (New Kensington, PA: Whitaker House, 1982), 54–56.

[33] Ibid., 55.

[34] revelation. (n.d.) Collins English Dictionary – Complete and Unabridged, 12th Edition 2014. (1991, 1994, 1998, 2000, 2003, 2006, 2007, 2009, 2011, 2014). Retrieved April 13 2022 from https://www.thefreedictionary.com/revelation

[35] grace - "G5485 - charis - Strong's Greek Lexicon (kjv)." Blue Letter Bible. Web. 14 Mar, 2022. <https://www.blueletterbible.org/lexicon/g5485/kjv/tr/0-1/>.

[36] fulfilled - "G4137 - plēroō - Strong's Greek Lexicon (kjv)." Blue Letter Bible. Web. 17 Mar, 2022. <https://www.blueletterbible.org/lexicon/g4137/kjv/tr/0-1/>.

About the Author

Dr. Ken Stewart is a prominent figure in the Christian community, with almost 60 years of experience in ministry and education. He is a respected author, pastor, and educator whose teachings have impacted countless individuals and families across the United States and beyond.

Born and raised in Arkansas, Dr. Stewart had an early calling to ministry. He attended Brite Divinity School at Texas Christian University in Fort Worth, Texas, where he received his Master of Divinity degree. He completed his Doctor of Ministry degree from the same institution, solidifying his knowledge and passion for serving the Lord.

Dr. Stewart began his ministry as a pastor, serving several churches in Texas and Oklahoma. He quickly gained a reputation for his straightforward and easy-to-understand teaching style, which drew people from all walks of life to his congregations.

Over time, Dr. Stewart's ministry expanded beyond the church walls. He became a sought-after speaker, travelling across the United States and abroad to share his knowledge and experience with others. He has spoken at countless conferences, retreats, and seminars, inspiring and educating audiences of all ages and backgrounds.

In addition to his work as a pastor and speaker, Dr. Stewart is also an accomplished author. He has written 16 books covering various topics related to the Christian faith. His writing is engaging, thought-provoking, and inspiring, and he has helped countless individuals and families grow in their faith.

One of Dr. Stewart's most recent books, "The New Covenant Psalm: Psalm 91 in the Light of the New Testament," offers a fresh perspective on one of the Bible's most beloved Psalms. The Psalm focuses on dealing with fear. Dr. Stewart provides practical insights on trusting God for protection and safety in a world filled with violence and danger. The book has been well-received by readers and has helped many find peace and security in their daily lives.

Now Dr. Stewart is introducing the newest addition to his library of work. This book titled "The Holy Spirit in the Life of Jesus" is the first of a series of books he has planned dealing with different facets of the work of the Holy Spirit. Other volumes will cover the work of the Holy Spirit in the ministry of Jesus and the ministry of the disciples. Finally, he has plans to write about the work and ministry of the Holy Spirit in the church today. This series of books is like no other material available on these subjects. You will want to own and read all of them.

Dr. Stewart's ministry has also focused on family relationships. He understands that many marital problems are caused by financial difficulties. To help couples navigate these challenges, he enrolled in the Graduate Business Center of Florida Tech in St. Petersburg, Florida, to study Financial Planning. He completed his training at NSU in Broken Arrow, OK. Having gained this knowledge, Dr. Stewart acquired the necessary licenses and started his own business, spanning 18 states and managing retirement plans for approximately 400 clients.

Dr. Stewart's extensive experience in ministry, education, and financial planning has made him a trusted advisor and mentor to many. His teachings are grounded in the Word of God and reflect his deep understanding of the human experience. His writing is accessible and inspiring. His insights into faith and Christian living have helped countless individuals and families find hope, healing, and peace.

In all his work, Dr. Stewart remains committed to serving the Lord and sharing His message of love, grace, and redemption with the world. He continues to write, speak, and mentor, inspiring and encouraging others to grow in their faith and deepen their relationship with God.

Empowering
Believers to
do the Works
of Jesus!

To Receive
Your Enrollment Form
Contact Us At:
tulsaholyspiritschool@gmail.com

Mailing Address:
PO Box 470492
Tulsa, OK 74147

In-Person Classes
Sunday Sessions International
6808 S Memorial Dr #110
Tulsa, OK 74133

Online Classes
shs.drkenstewart.com

PUBLISHING

P O Box 470492

Tulsa, OK 74147

www.ingramcontent.com/pod-product-compliance
Lightning Source LLC
Chambersburg PA
CBHW052034020726
47501CB00004B/1399